GUARDIANS OF THE ANCESTORS

Guardians of the Ancestors

Spirit Voyager Book One

R. DE WOLF

Rhythmic Weave Books an Imprint of R. de Wolf

A catalogue record for this book is available from the National Library of New Zealand.

Soft Cover ISBN 978-1-99-118965-3

Logo: www.vecteezy.com/freevector/ornament Ornament Vectors by Vecteezy

Published in New Zealand by
Rhythmic Weave Books
An imprint of R. de Wolf
PO Box 438
Gisborne 4040

Second Edition
First Printing, 2024
Australia

To my tīpuna, who made me who I am.

Books by R. de Wolf

The Future Weavers Book Two

Brothers in Whalesong Book Three

The Goodness Algorithm

Poetry In a Pear Tree

Poetry In a Pohutukawa

Anthology Appearances:

Katuhi Rawhiti: *A Celebration of East Coast Writers* - short story Crushed Violet

Kaituhi Rāwhiti Two: *Weaving of Words* - short stories The Hollow Mother, Whale Brothers

Ngā Kupu Wero *(Penguin)* - Whakautu

Chapter 1

For Marama, the day started like any other. Blue sky, sun shining and the lapping hiss of waves on the sand.

The girl swayed like a palm frond, dancing in the breeze, enjoying the warmth through closed eyelids.

"Ugghh," she shrieked.

The slap of cold water jolted her eyes open. It was Tane, her best friend, grinning like a shark. Pleased with his prank and her squeal, he sprinted for the lagoon. His pink-soled feet flashed, and arms and legs pumped furiously to remove himself from the retaliation in hot pursuit.

When Tane reached the edge of the lagoon, he could feel the stitch clawing at his side, and he doubled over, clutching his puku (stomach.) Tane tried to stifle his giggles until he could suck in enough air.

The coconut whizzed past his ear and cracked against the tree behind him, showering him with juice and pulpy flesh. Marama crowed and whooped at the result of her catapult. He was faster, but she'd run a shorter route to the lagoon. One that cut out many corners of the path, and her reward; she'd totally surprised him.

"Call yourself a warrior," she taunted. "I know fish who are better runners than you and coconuts who are smarter."

She poked out her tongue, waggled her fingers on either side of her head and laughed before dashing to the water. Tane exploded from his crouch, his pain forgotten and launched himself at her, bowling both into the water with his momentum.

The water enfolded them as they plummeted toward the bottom, cooling their sweat-streaked skin and inflammatory words and deeds. As they kicked for the surface, they grinned in unison. Gasping for air after the exertion of their morning antics. She rolled onto her back, eyes closed again.

Tane tread water, watching her as his stomach tightened. Something had changed between them. He dreamed about swimming naked with her last night. What kind of a best friend am I, he wondered. She was still a child. Her body was lithe and supple as a boy, and her breasts were just beginning to bud, unlike some girls her age who already had men and children.

Tane observed she wasn't beautiful like the village girls with their liquid eyes, seductive smiles, and curvy bodies. They were already batting their eyelids at him and enticing him with swaying hips. He'd been unable to resist their allure. Tane enjoyed the physical pleasure of their games but hadn't chosen a regular partner.

Something was always missing, disappointing in a way. Of course, he couldn't talk about these feelings with his best friend as usual, so he existed in confusion. He resigned to the village men's popular belief that women are impossible to understand.

She splashed water on his face. "Why are you frowning, Tane? Is the pain of thought troubling your tiny brain?"

The broad smile blunted the barb of her words. He looked at her face. A strong face with a straight nose, much sharper than everyone else's. Generous lips but not fleshy like his and a crooked tooth that overlapped the one next to it on the left side. Her face was lean, with a firm chin for a girl, and a scar ran from her forehead through her left eyebrow. The result of one of their misadventures, but her eyes made her stand out. They seemed to look right through him, straight into his mind. And they were green.

Her father washed up on the island's shore and had been taken in by her grandmother and mother. Everyone said he had red hair and blue eyes, so he supposed she got her unusual features from her father. She was not beautiful, but not ordinary. Tane had been alarmed to discover that the Chief's youngest son was fascinated by her.

Marama's grandmother held high status as the village spirit guide and healer; with her daughter gone, she'd taken her grandchild as her pupil. When they were children, everyone teased and bullied the girl. As the biggest, strongest and fastest runner, he'd taken it upon himself to protect her. In the process, he'd discovered how clever she was, and they had become best friends - the pranksters of the village. They often incurred the wrath of this or that child and occasionally punishment from their elders when they went too far. They lived a wild and joyous childhood filled with adventures.

He looked at her with an earnest, considered gaze. If he were honest with himself, he couldn't stand the thought of her sharing her life, laughter, and insights with anyone else. He also couldn't imagine his life without her in it every day.

Aue! (an exclamation of dismay) My life is so confusing, thought Tane. Had he just admitted he wanted her for himself? Was she haunting his dreams because the rest of him already knew he wanted to be more than her best friend?

She quirked one eyebrow at him, another little trick of hers that he couldn't do.

"Well, what is it? You are not pining after that moon face, Hine, are you? I have seen you two smooching when you think nobody is looking, or is it the girl from last week that lives in the next village?"

Her mouth was set in a hard line, and she looked peeved. Tane grinned; maybe she didn't like the thought of him with anyone else. She didn't seem pleased with his romantic choices.

The world stopped. Air thickened. The water between them subsided. Their faces almost touched. He could feel her breath on his chin but realised he was not breathing. His body was taught. Poised to dive off the cliff into the ocean.

Tane felt feverish, like when he'd been ill, heart hammering in his chest. Blood pulsing in his temples. The girl touched his lips, claiming his kiss, heart, and love with confident ownership that defied her trembling insides.

The tension of their confusion-laden puberty was released like water breaching a dam. It washed them away to a place where time was irrelevant and they'd never dreamed of going together. Only they existed in a glorious sunny moment that neither wanted to end.

It did not matter that they were clumsy or inexperienced. They found their way, trusting each other and testing their newfound senses.

Their bodies knew what to do, so their instincts took over, as other creatures do when the call to mate is urgent.

They lay together in the shallows of the lagoon, cradled in each other's arms. They were jubilant, sated and filled with wonder at their new relationship. Neither spoke. Nobody wanted to spoil the perfection of the moment.

Then Tane startled.

"I can hear voices—a lot of voices, like whispering or bees swarming. Here, take this reed and go into the shadows. No need for the whole village to tell your Nani we were cavorting naked in the lagoon. Stay here, and don't move; I will come and get you when they are gone."

Marama flushed pink and stifled a giggle but did as he asked and paddled to the far end of the lagoon, bobbing under with only the reed poking out.

She and Tane could stay like this for hours. Their competitions were ferocious battles of will and the source of the odd beating when they failed to show up for chores.

Tane stole to the other side of the lagoon and peeked around the trunk of a coconut tree. For the second time, his heart stopped. Only this time, what he saw left him trembling.

The voices he heard were not those of villagers. He saw a large, heavily armed raiding party from another island. Tane had to warn the village but threw an anxious look toward the shadows.

Marama would be safe. Clever and resourceful, she would stay hidden, but he needed to fly. Tane backtracked stealthily, skirting the lagoon under the cover of the trees, and then he ran.

He ran with all his heart and took Marama's shortcuts.

"Hi Tane," the children playing called.

"Go home, go home now," he shouted.

When he reached the first adults, he cried.

"Raiders, raiders at the lagoon are coming, many, well-armed."

People were shocked and stopped what they were doing as the message sank in. They blanched and ran for shelter or weapons. By now, Tane was almost spent, but someone ran ahead to get the Chief, who sprinted to meet Tane.

"How many, Tane?"

"There were already 40 or so on the beach, and still men coming around the point. They have spears and clubs. Prepare for a fight."

The Chief ordered all men and battle-trained boys to arm themselves and asked his healer to take the women and children to the hiding cave. Tane saw the girl's grandmother looking for her. Nani ordered the women and children to leave everything except food and water. Her frown betrayed her worry over her missing charge.

Tane felt a pang of guilt but he didn't have time to speak with her. He needed his weapons and to drink. Catch his breath for the coming clash, and listen to instructions.

A runner left for the next village, but they were un-likely to arrive in time. So they could be outnumbered, maybe heavily outnumbered. The Chief would be formu-lating a battle plan. The raiders must have paddled in on the high tide, under the cover of darkness, to avoid the lookouts. There was no moon last night. The enemy was rested and had caught them off guard.

The Chief gathered his men around him, 62 counting the older boys. They threw mats over their food storage pits, hoping some would fall in when they charged. They left tools scattered where they'd been dropped, a sign of hasty departure. Dividing his force, a third of them were concealed in the village, while the Chief led the remain-ing warriors to circle the village. They would attack the invaders from the rear once they entered and trap them inside an inner and outer circle.

It was a good plan, but it relied on the enemy charging. If this was not the case, they needed to work their way behind them. It was a more complex task as the enemy would have scouts. The Chief frowned as his mind ticked through strategic options and the risks of each one to his men.

The breeze sighed in alert ears. It was a sigh of fear and despair as the men waited for the attack, hoping it was a Tane prank but knowing nobody joked about invasions.

When they came, they came silently on the main path. There was no charge. They halted in disciplined ranks, and Tane's hopes sank as a lone scout entered cautiously. The Chief placed his index finger over his lips.

Each man knew where his flanking warriors were hiding so they would have a line of communication.

The scout threw the mats off the pits with a flourish, grinning at his raiding party as he bent down, examining the melee of footprints. Many prints were heading out of the village where the women, children and warriors departed as the Chief had planned.

The scout continued his tour of the village, avoiding anywhere an ambush might await. While lifting lids of baskets with his spear, a loud belch sounded from inside a storehouse.

Quick as a sea snake, the scout's hand struck inside and yanked a yelping boy out by the hair. It was Piki.

His face, covered in fruit juice and soft coconut pulp, clumped in the corners of his mouth.

"What have we got here? A squealing little piggy – oink, oink! Can't wait to eat you," he sneered, widening his eyes and protruding his tongue to scare the boy further. It worked, and Piki started to sob. "Where is everyone, little pig?" the scout asked while twisting his ear, eliciting another squeal from Piki.

"They all ran away to hide," he sobbed, "I thought I could stay here, hide, and nobody would miss all the good things to eat they left behind. I never get to eat the best fruit or coconut. Please don't eat me. I can show you where all the good food is."

"It looks like it already found its way into your fat puku little pig." The warriors all laughed. "So, little pig, can you show us where everybody went?" Piki's face was streaked with tears and snot, hiccupping out sobs as he nodded animatedly.

"Can I, can I just put something on my feet? There will be sharp rocks." The scout raised his eyebrows and laughed again.

"Of course, little pig, can't have my dinner cut, dirty and bruised before I am ready to eat it," he growled, smacking his lips.

Piki hobbled to a doorway to get his footwear. The scout followed him, and the invaders trickled into the village, visibly relaxed and enjoying the show put on by a terrified Piki.

Tane held his breath. Piki picked up his footwear, but as he turned and regarded the approaching warriors, he peed his pants like a baby. The invaders pointed and laughed, some crying with amusement at 'little Piggy's' bravery.

Piki bound his footwear on his urine-stained feet. He pivoted gracefully like a dancer and slashed the jugular of the laughing scout before plunging an obsidian dagger into his stomach and ripping it upward, screaming his war cry.

The scout's face puckered in disbelief, his bravado ebbing with his blood. Piki's battle cry was the catalyst for the hidden warriors. They leapt out of huts, surprising the enemy and engaging them in fierce hand-to-hand combat.

The invaders realised they had superior numbers, so they encircled the fighters to wear them out and minimise unnecessary loss of their men. As the invading circle tightened around the village defenders, the warriors hiding in the undergrowth crept forward. They stood poised, waiting for the signal. The Chief raised his spear high. They prepared to charge. He axed his club through the air, and they stealthily stormed the village, forming an outer circle with the invaders caught between the two groups of defenders.

They were still outnumbered, but their battle cries startled the enemy for the second time as they joined the fight. That element of surprise helped even the odds.

Fighting was ferocious and bloody. It wasn't the normal village raid to steal food without getting caught or to kidnap a maiden often happy to run off with her lover. This was a fight for life and death. Battle lust overtook them, staining the soil with sweat and blood.

The invader's leader rallied a group of warriors, and they advanced toward the Chief.

Tane saw the enemy's intent. Their Chief was surrounded by the fallen bodies of the enemy. His prowess as a warrior had not waned during a time of peace. The Chief practised with his weapons daily. He drilled the young warriors and took his fighting men on exhausting runs, swims, paddles and hikes. His body was slicked with sweat as well-trained muscles rippled with the joy of practised movement. Tane rallied some of their own men without breaking the line.

Tane's father died in battle when Tane was a baby, and the Chief his mentor, the only father he'd ever known.

The invading leader was cunning; the tide was turning against them. He decided to rip the men to pieces by killing the Chief.

Tane needed to hurry, so he screamed a warning over the battle din. He saw his Chief flick his eyes over the unfolding battle. Clock the advancing threat. The Chief plucked a spear from a body behind him. Hurled it at the invaders running toward him. His aim was true. The first man dropped in his tracks, impeding the men behind him and buying valuable seconds for Tane and his force.

They rushed into the gap before their Chief and encircled him to provide protection from all sides with their bodies and weapons. Tane was young, but he took the fight to the advancing forces, turning the tables and urging the village warriors to claim the mana of defeating the leader of the invaders. The battle raged - intense.

The villagers were defending their homes and families. Their muscles and weapons answered the call for their tīpuna (ancestors) to take up arms against their enemies with them.

Their Chief was now in formation with his men, his weapons singing death. They whistled in harmony with the flowing movement of his body, and the invader's resolve wavered before his advance. Only their leader danced a challenge. Muscles bulged in a defiant and untiring response, boasting of his youth, warrior credentials, and vicious ambition.

The enemy leader hurled his spear straight and flat at the Chief to win the day. His aim was accurate. Only Tane's hastily raised taiaha deflected the invader's spear from its objective. The leader screamed his frustration and launched a running attack at Tane.

Tane crouched on the ground, his arm dead and limp from intercepting the spear. He surged to his feet and launched at his attacker, whacking his ankles with his weapon to catch him off guard. The leader tumbled to the ground, but years of training, muscle memory and reflex enabled him to roll in a fluid motion. He was on his feet again behind Tane in a heartbeat.

The blow fell, swift and heavy. All the venom of the leader's disappointment was released. The light that was Tane faded in this world. His body lay broken. Bloody upon the ground, his slowing heart calling for his lost love.

The leader glanced up, wearing a wry smirk of satisfaction at killing the boy who turned the battle. His glance also absorbed that his men were in retreat, and the village Chief was advancing on him with murder in his eyes. He longed to fight the Chief, but the raid had not gone to plan, and his men's retreat exposed him. His father had taught him a leader must know when to accept a loss, save his men and live to fight another day.

The bitterness of defeat was bile in his mouth, and his pride smarted as he acknowledged a fat boy, an adolescent warrior and an ageing Chief had routed his dominant, more experienced forces.

The leader channelled his frustration into a call for retreat and ran for his life, rapidly passing his men. Leading them to the safety of their canoes. He doubted the chase would be in earnest. They had wounded and dead to tend to, but he pushed his men mercilessly to keep up the pace. Partially to give them enough of a head start to launch their waka (canoe) if they were pursued and to practice the manoeuvre for when their lives depended on their speed. He also wanted to punish them for their weakness and the defeat.

As the leader reached the lagoon, his breath coming hard, he stopped. The head of a water nymph surfaced in the lagoon. Water streamed off her hair and skin, or was it a young woman? Their eyes locked. Her green eyes were alarmed. Then she was gone. This was not the time to take prisoners, but the leader was fascinated.

"I am Mako. I will return to claim you. You are mine," he shouted.

A promise, Marama, didn't want to hear.

Chapter 2

The girl shuddered in the lagoon with a premonition of death and despair. Mako, the leader's face, was imprinted behind her eyes. She returned the reed to her lips, disturbed the water as little as possible, and found a comfortable position to stand and take air away from the lagoon's edge. The fleeing invaders crashed through the undergrowth, pounding the path from the village, their retreat as noisy as their approach had been stealthy.

The noise faded, but the girl remained in the lagoon; she had no wish to encounter fierce strangers. Tane or her Nani would look for her when it was safe.

"Marama! Marama, are you here?"

It was her Nani who had come looking for her. Once again, she emerged from the lagoon with water streaming from her face and hair; this time, her skin was puckered and bumpy from hiding submerged.

"I'm sorry, Nani, I missed my lesson, but Tane heard noises and asked me to hide until he came. I hope it wasn't another one of his stupid jokes. Nani, are you alright? What happened?"

The kuia (elderly woman) hastily blinked tears from her eyes, but it was too late. The girl saw, and a sense of foreboding hung like a stone in her breast.

"Aue, aue, we were attacked in the village by a raiding party, and a bloody battle was fought. My child, if Tane had not warned us before they arrived, we would've all been slaughtered," she said.

"So now Tane is a hero. Trust him, I will never hear the end of it! Nobody was hurt, were they?"

Nani's face contorted, and she shook her head in abject sadness.

"We lost four men, and many others are wounded. I am sorry, Marama, there is no easy way to tell you this: Tane fell in battle and dwells with our ancestors in the next life. He left us, cloaked in glory. He saved the life of our Chief and turned the outcome of the raid and battle. His purpose in this life must have been fulfilled, and the Gods and our tīpuna called him home. I'm so sorry, my child. I know how you loved him."

Tears welled in the girl's eyes and slid down her face. She was numb inside. Nani dried her brusquely, but the girl only felt the pain building in her chest, radiating throughout her body, until it burst forth in an anguished primaeval scream.

It couldn't be true. How could this happen? They had only just found and acknowledged their love. Just a few moments ago, Tane was in her arms, his breath in her ears and on her skin, the warmth of his body against hers.

"Why? Why? Why? This is not fair," she wailed, head in hands. The girl fell to her knees and screamed at the sky. Consumed with anger and despair. She pounded her fists on the ground until they were bloody and lacerated from the shell fragments in the sand. Nani let the girl spew her grief in a raging torrent before gathering her in her arms. Allowing her to completely unravel in the embrace that had comforted and loved her unstintingly during her short but tumultuous life.

Marama had been named for the full moon she was born under. The moon shed silvery light on her face as she drew her first breath and blessed her with a mind as swift and mercurial as its beams. Nani watched the sleeping girl fondly with a furrowed brow.

It was such a harrowing life for one so young. Marama had lost her father, mother and now her best friend, first love most likely and future mate. The bond between herself and the child was intense from the beginning. They were not only a grandmother and granddaughter sharing the pain of loss.

They were also a teacher and pupil, friends, competitors and adversaries intellectually. However, one strong relationship wasn't a lot for a young woman. Nani had welcomed the friendship with Tane, even though their mischief-making sometimes drove her mad or caused a bit of grief and embarrassment. It had been wonderful to see her behaving as a child should. The reality was that she thought as an adult more often than not. That meant she found most of the children foolish. Combined with her sharp tongue, that hadn't made her popular.

Now, Tane was gone. Suddenly, Marama was left with his killer's promise to return and claim her. This was not something that Marama could comprehend.

The village children had constantly taunted Marama, 'You are ugly,' they'd tease when Tane wasn't in earshot. Now, she was unusual and striking, unique, if not beautiful. This attracted attention whether she saw it, liked it or not.

Her grief was raw. A few days prior, Nani caught her wading into the sea when a rip pulled everything out beyond the reef. She only returned to the shore when she realised her Nani was wading out with her and would most likely drown.

In truth, for a fleeting moment, Nani wondered if it was the right choice for them both. Marama was her world, all she had left. But hers was a well-lived life, and Marama's had scarcely begun. Who knew what lay ahead for the girl. She was robust and could probably survive most things if she survived this. Still, when Nani departed to the next world, Marama would be alone. Somehow, Nani must find Marama a reason to live. Nani wrapped her cloak around her shoulders and consulted the ancestors in the stars. She needed to find an answer fast.

Nani frowned, displeased at failing to interest her granddaughter in living again. The days turned into moon cycles, and Marama was shrinking into herself, willing her lungs to stop breathing or her heart to cease beating its tattoo of life.

At first, Nani was patient and understanding. Comforting the woman-child with soothing words and soft hands. Then, she became frustrated with Marama when she refused to eat, bathe, or do the daily chores that life demanded.

Last night, Nani's temper erupted in a desperate effort to make an impression on Marama.

"I am an old woman! You expect me to fetch water, do all the cooking and cleaning and tend the sick while looking after you? Aue! How could I have raised such a selfish child?"

She rarely raised her voice to the child, and Marama's eyes widened in surprise. Then she curled into a ball underneath her cloak and stopped breathing, hands cradling her head. The guilt would have been unbearable for Nani if it hadn't been planned to elicit a reaction.

This morning, Nani changed tactics again. Marama was a clever girl who mulled over problems with sound logic and a sense of reasoning. She was proud of her intelligence and strength, so Nani would plant seeds and see if they germinated while Marama skulked in the dark.

"Marama, you must eat. If Mako returns to claim you as he promised, he will be victorious. You are no match for such a man in this state. The village will suffer. I will most likely be killed, and Tane's death will go unavenged. We need to have a plan, or we are all lost. Think about it."

Marama heard the words reverberating in her ears and mind. However, Marama replayed her happiest moments with her father before he left. Then, her mother, before she left, never returned and, most painfully, with Tane, who was now dead.

She had no more tears to cry, but her mind screamed to end this. Everyone who loved her left her or died. Only Nani endured, and she was already ancient. She would also depart this world, and Marama would be alone.

Marama would not have to endure the pain and suffering of more loss if she died now. She just couldn't take anymore. A lone tear rolled down her nose, trailing a salty path to her downturned mouth. 'I am nothing', she thought. 'No good to anyone, why can't I just die? Why couldn't I have died in battle with Tane or at least saved him?'

"If there are Gods, I hate you all," she whispered, "you are all useless."

A kernel of anger was forming inside her, providing respite from the depressive melancholy that had seeped into her bones, sapping her will to live.

Her heart felt as if it had been shattered. Bound together several times, smashed by a boulder into thousands of tiny pieces, but it still beat. Why? In that moment of self-pity, she heard a whisper in her ear. Marama's eyes flew open, startled. It was Tane's voice, dripping with sarcasm.

"I leave you alone for a few days, and you become a snivelling mess. You are pathetic," Tane scoffed. "You need to get off your bony little arse and look after Nani, for she is right. My murderer will return for you, and imagine how upset he will be to find this skinny excuse for a girl in your place. He'll be so angry he will slaughter everyone in the village. If you truly ever loved me, you will avenge me and finish my work."

Then he was gone. I must be going crazy, Marama thought, hearing voices in her head. But it was not voices - it was Tane's voice, Tane's words, Tane's thoughts. A reason to live?

Nani burst into the hut with a very pregnant woman, quite old to bear a child by village standards. The sweat on her brow and the blood on her legs told Marama all was not well.

Marama's heart lurched, broken or not. She knew she should be helping. Nani's eyesight was not good, and she was becoming frail. There was work to do. Marama threw off the cloak and her malaise and rushed to the fire, stirring the embers to warm the water in the gourd beside it. She ran to the supply of herbs and roots in the hut, asking Nani what she wanted first.

Nani blinked and issued rapid instructions, allowing herself an inward smile. She knew Marama was soft-hearted, especially with the women and children; healing was an undeniable calling for her. Marama possessed skills far beyond her years, and her voracity for learning and thinking amazed the kuia.

This morning, however, Nani had resorted to her own healing forte, the spiritual and pleaded with her ancestors to intervene to save her granddaughter's life. She was sure her grandmother was there and had also felt Tane's presence. At the same time, she meditated on the beach at sunrise, and she returned feeling comforted and optimistic.

Shortly after, the woman Kura's labour began, closer to their whare (house) than Kura's own home. Apparently, Kura felt compelled to visit Nani, even though she was not due to give birth yet. Nani gave a silent nod of thanks to her spiritual helpers. They were much wiser than she, and Nani rushed the woman inside to be greeted by the reaction she prayed for from Marama.

Marama mixed the potion for the pain; it was a potent mix. She got Kura to drink it all, sip by sip, while comforting and cooling her flushed face and getting her to breathe through the pain of the contractions.

Nani watched Marama with pride. Her calm demeanour and unflappable efficiency were undiminished in a crisis. Nani cleaned the blood away and staunched the flow as best she could, applying a topical anaesthetic to the external tear. Now, her fingers were busy probing inside to see if the baby was alive and in the correct position.

The baby was warm, but the contractions weren't pushing it out as fast as they should have, and the top of its head was red. Nani felt the umbilical cord wrapped around the baby's neck, pulling tighter with each contraction.

"The baby is alive, Kura, but don't push with the next contraction. Marama, come here, please. I need you to help deliver the baby."

Nani handed Marama the obsidian knife that she used for surgery. It was always sterilised and ready for emergencies. Nani signalled to Marama what the problem was so as not to panic the already distressed mother. By now, Kura's sisters had arrived, and Nani instructed them to sit on each side and hold her.

The pain potion was taking effect, but saving the baby would be painful. Nani used her gnarled but experienced fingers to expose the baby's neck and the tightening umbilical cord to Marama. Kura screamed, biting down hard on the compacted sponge her sister had placed between her teeth. Marama used deft fingers to cut the umbilical cord swiftly and free the baby to enter the world. And enter he did. In a rush of contractions, his mother expelled him from her womb, crying in pain and relief before passing out.

As Marama cradled the baby, she saw he was no longer breathing. His lips were a greyish blue. She opened his mouth, clearing his airways, pinched his nose and blew into his tiny lungs. Just as she'd seen her father do when he saved one of the children from drowning in the surf. After a few breaths, the baby's chest moved up and down. He coughed and then gave out an almighty wail, angrily waving his fists in the air. Nani and Marama looked at each other and smiled. They had done this together many times, assisting a new life.

They wrapped the baby and lay him on his mother's chest for the comfort of her familiar presence and smell and to tell her body to hurry with his milk. His Aunts clucked and cooed over him, soothing him with their warm hands and cleaning him up.

Nani and Marama turned their attention to Kura. They could see external tearing as the baby's head had been pushing for some time, inhibited by the umbilical cord.

Marama took up her needle and thread while Nani checked for internal bleeding and prepared for the after-birth, which they would bury in a sacred place to thank the ancestors. Everything seemed to be alright, but they would need to bathe the wounds quickly to stop any infection. Marama had prepared the cleansing herbs in a stone bowl and washed the wound before stitching the torn flesh.

Another clean, and the rest would be up to Kura. Marama hoped that Kura had not lost too much blood and had the strength to fight off infection. She and the baby were lucky they were almost at Nani's whare. No doubt Nani would be giving thanks to her spirits as usual. Marama had always been dubious about the ability to commune with people who had entered the next world until today.

Again, Marama experienced the gurgling well of Tane's laughter in her head and his voice teasing her. "You know nothing. You only think you are clever, but well done with the baby, my love." Then he was gone again. Marama smiled to herself. Nani was right, she thought.

Tane is still with me. Her whole body was suffused with love, and she felt the same tingling on her skin when Tane held her in his arms and stroked her face and limbs. For the first time since Tane died, Marama wanted to live. She almost giggled and thought she was losing her mind but felt comforted by the voice in her head.

Much to Nani's delight, Marama resumed her chores and healing duties as if she'd never left them. In fact, Nani observed a new vigour and sense of urgency in all Marama's activities. It was as if she tried to make up for the days she had lost. Nani's observations were as astute as ever. Marama knew she must recover her lost strength and make up for being so useless and childish in her grief. She ran everywhere, even for pleasure, up the hills and on the sand as she'd seen the warriors in training doing. She counted the numbers her father had taught her as she climbed the trees to get coconuts, striving to climb ever faster. Her pounding of vegetables, grains or herbs was ferocious. Nani feared she would break her bowls and pounding implements, but instead of cuffing her ear as she might have, she let Marama vent her emotions and train her muscles. The girl had become leaner and wirier than ever; her muscle tone put some warriors to shame, and her strength was evident in the loads she carried for work and playing with the children.

Marama went about life more like a boy than a girl. Her gathering and foraging skills were the envy of many other households. Nani's status as a healer and spiritual advisor who could read the moon cycles and stars afforded them the pick of food the village men provided when they returned from hunting and fishing.

The fact that they took so little raised their status even further. Although women did not hunt and weapons were for men only, Marama's father had made fish traps and taught his small daughter how to set and maintain them. Marama had also made traps for birds and small animals that lived on the island.

Their catch was sufficient for them, and they often shared with other families. Some questions were posed about whether the trapping was hunting and whether it should be permitted. Nani and the Chief pointed out that no weapons were involved, that parts of the fish and animals were used for healing and that the village benefited from the activity. The following moon cycle, Marama assisted other women and girls in making their own traps. It became an accepted gathering activity.

Marama and Nani also maintained their own whare. Replacing thatch and weaving beautiful spiritual patterns into their mats and wall hangings. The villagers knew Nani and Marama were clever and self-sufficient. They added to the status of the village.

Other villages sent runners for help from Nani and Marama, especially for high-status individuals and childbirth. This knock-on effect made their settlement desirable for girls to take a partner. The girl's parents would know their daughter would have the best care when producing mokopuna (grandchildren).

This was a good outcome, and over time, the strangeness of Marama's pale-skinned, red-head, blue-eyed father and his golden, green-eyed daughter were accepted as a gift that provided innovation and status.

The people had never found the sight of Marama's unusual colouring out of the ordinary because she was a child growing up in their midst. They only remembered if people who hadn't seen her came from elsewhere. When it happened, they delighted in the gaping and surreptitious glances that often followed. It was a great source of amusement for everyone. The behaviour put visitors on the back foot when trading. Staring was considered impolite, and many a hard bargain was struck on the back of casual comments that implied they'd noticed improper behaviour.

Only recently, Nani had noticed Tane was a bit more reserved around Marama and that the Chief's son mooched after her like a baby longing for its Mama's milk. Even some of the warriors were giving her a second glance. It surprised Nani, and she wasn't often surprised. When Marama's moon bleeding began, Nani took stock of the girl and decided they still had time to discuss choosing a man.

Marama was still childish in many ways. She behaved like a boy and had never expressed any interest in boys or men other than Tane.

Nani supposed her first mating experience would probably be with Tane, and they might make their whare together. Tane matured early. Girls from all over the islands sought him out. Nani would have been happy with either outcome as she knew the boy well, had bought him into the world and knew he would be smart enough for her independent, unusual grandchild.

Marama was not beautiful in a traditional way. She was different. Being clever, a good provider and an adept healer afforded her status. Alas, fate intervened, and Marama and Tane would not have the choice or chance to build a life together.

Nani glanced up from her weaving, alerted by the stillness in the whare. Marama sat on her knees and feet, frowning and staring into space. She turned to Nani as the old woman's gaze settled on her.

"Nani, how long does a warrior raiding party take to recover from losses and prepare for another raid?"

Nani regarded her grandchild, alert. It was a well-considered and astute question. Marama's grasp of the masculine world, mind and adult thinking was keen.

"It's a question our Chief is also pondering, Marama. We discussed the tides and the moon cycle just last week. He's also considering the elements of lost men, paddlers, provisions and duties. How a Chief reacts to the failure and adds that to the wounded pride, smarting and eating at the heart and mind of a young, overly ambitious warrior.

"Is Mako a new chief?"

"He thinks not, more likely the son of an older Chief looking to stake his claim as the next chief. Mako was well-fed, highly skilled and carried impressive weapons.

We don't know where exactly they came from. Definitely another island, but not our nearest neighbours as we didn't recognise any of them. I have shared your account of the promise to return and take you, Marama. We fear this was not an idle threat from such a man. Our Chief knows that he is a thinking warrior as he is himself. Mako will be settling on a strategy to take you, most probably petitioning his chief to take revenge for the death of the men in the raiding party and to assuage his wounded ego. An unfortunate pull of the tides brought them here. An undesirable design of fate. You were deep in thought, Marama. How do your thoughts run?"

"I fear you and our Chief are both wise and correct, Nani. I try to put myself into his head and imagine what I would do in his place."

Nani raised her brows in response. It was an unusual point of view for a girl who had never seen or been in a battle.

"I would be furious and embarrassed at the same time. I couldn't rest until I returned and put things right. I would, however, put more thought into the raid next time. Mako's intelligence will war with pride and win the day as it did when he minimised his losses and withdrew his men. He knows the village will prepare for a possible raid, so the element of surprise has been lost. I would discuss my strategy with experienced warriors to see if they could add anything to enhance my chances. I would land on our island in a different place but maybe apply the same tactic of arriving under the cover of darkness with no moon. They will know the lay of the land and our village better next time. They could sneak into our midst at night while we sleep. The best idea would be to wait until we have grown complacent and thoughts of their return are replaced by the worries of everyday life. I don't believe he will wait that long. If his father is the chief, he will have a difficult decision. He may not wish to tarnish the reputation of his chosen successor by waiting.

They may arrive with a more significant force if they have more fighting men, even young men in training. After all, our young men turned of the battle."

Marama paused, again staring into space as if looking for answers in the air. Nani recognised the posture she often adopted, as had her daughter, Marama's mother, when deep in thought or communing with the spirits.

Nani was pleased with Marama. She would share her thoughts with their Chief and see if they mesh with his own. Marama's ability to think like other people, turn problems over in her mind and look at them from different angles was a gift she inherited from her parents.

Her father loved to solve a problem and created many new tools during his time with them to improve the efficiency of their daily chores.

Nani thought Marama would have made an excellent boy and a strategic warrior or leader. Her mother was often frustrated that a woman's role involved so much cooking and cleaning. Like Marama, she'd also been an accomplished healer with her own status. Her strength enabled her to reset bones, remove teeth and deliver breech birth babies, so her renown as a healer was independent of her mother.

It was one of the reasons she'd been allowed to remain in quarantine with him on the outskirts when she'd taken Marama's father into her whare as her man. The presence of two healers in one place was an advantage for status. However, the price for Marama's mother would have been high, and there was some resentment that she chose such a strange man.

Marama ruminated on her thoughts. Her priority was the safety of Nani and her people, but the desire for revenge was a burning flame. She needed a plan and a good one.

If it was her that Mako wanted, and he had promised to claim her, this could be used to their advantage. What she really wanted was to discuss strategy with the Chief. However, she was painfully aware that she was a skinny girl with zero experience of battle or war.

Nani was often consulted due to her connection to the spirit world and the stars. Maybe she shouldn't have neglected her education in this area; she'd viewed the next realm as superstition. Marama had now experienced the spirits herself and could see the advantages of participating in decisions outside women's work. When Marama told her she'd heard Tane's voice and felt his presence, Nani had been unsurprised. Nani was a little smug about it and delighted Marama shared her gift of communing with the afterworld.

Marama's fishing, gathering, trapping, and healing work were satisfying. Sometimes, she envied the boys as she spied on them surreptitiously as they were receiving their weapons training. It was tapu (forbidden) for her to watch, but she had, and she practised with sticks and rocks when she was alone on the beach or up in the mountains. By her own reckoning, she was adequately skilled or better at the warrior exercises than some boys.

After so much loss and her strange appearance, Marama knew she could not afford to be weak or stupid if she wanted to survive. The pranks she and Tane played and the antics, with their incessant competitions, had really pushed the boundaries of what was acceptable. It taught them many lessons about assessing risks and the consequences of failure or getting caught. Occasionally, they had both taken a beating, each refusing to cry out in pain even though they knew the punishment would be worse.

Marama felt the warmth of Tane's arms and decided to sleep on the problem and look at options in the morning when her mind was uncluttered. Her thoughts were as bright and clear as the water in the lagoon. She drifted asleep and was again in the lagoon, blissfully cradled in Tane's arms.

After the evening meal, Nani arrived at the Chief's whare, and his family had retired. She materialised out of the dark as he sat before the fire, staring into the flames and sharpening his whalebone club with loving strokes. The striking edge was sharp and brutal, its beauty belying the damage it could cause. The Chief's eyes flicked to Nani, but his muscles relaxed when he saw who it was.

He motioned for Nani to sit and asked if she wanted a warm drink. Nani smiled, produced a mixture of herbs and aromatic seeds from a pouch under her cloak, and steeped them in a coconut shell. The fragrance was both sweet and spicy. Nani proffered a cup to the Chief first, and he smiled. Nani knew he liked the taste of the tea almost as much as he enjoyed the relief from the pains in his body.

Perhaps his longevity as the Chief might be attributed to this old woman who healed many wounds and boosted his body with a plethora of potions and tisanes.

Nani was old now, and he was happy her granddaughter was as accomplished as her lost mother, for Nani and the village's sake.

Nani's hair was grey when he was a boy. He had no idea how old Nani was. Her father had been the chief then, and her brother the next leader, but her brother disappeared while fishing in his outrigger, so he became 'Chief' - it was now his name.

Chief was becoming old; his body and reflection in the pools did not lie, and he needed to pave the way for his successor. Tane had died so young. Despite his boisterous nature, he'd been a natural warrior and leader and undoubtedly more of a strategic thinker than any of his sons. He'd hoped Tane might support one of his sons and take on the role of chief himself one day.

Being the son of a chief did not automatically qualify you to lead; you needed to have prowess in battle and respect from your men and the village when it came to making decisions. Of course, when your father was chief, you observed at close hand what the position involved and had access to the best of everything that the village could offer. His sons lacked a creative mind that could find a path through the many obstacles and challenges that life laid out before them.

If only Nani had been young enough to take as a wife. They might have produced a formidable leader with strength and intelligence to spare. His sons had not made much of an impression in the battle. They fought well but with mechanically drilled bodies. In contrast, Tane could see the fight unfolding. Piki had the intelligence to improve the distraction when the scout searched cautiously. As the chief, he never would have asked the boy to wet himself. Piki had thought of it and done it without regard for his embarrassment. He'd done everything he could to save his people, gained the advantage and despatched a wary man twice his age.

The Chief decided to spend more time training Piki, who had shown courage and skill under pressure when it mattered. He was still Chief because he did the job best, even with his ageing body. Had Tane not saved him, he doubted he could have matched the invader's leader in one-on-one combat unless he had managed to outthink him. It was not a comforting thought when the invaders' return was inevitable.

Nani didn't come to his home fire unless she had something important to say. So, he laid aside his weapon to concentrate on the often cryptic words she delivered from their ancestors. The old woman had, of course, been conferring with the spirit world. At the moment, he could do with the guidance of his tīpuna. The village's fate may well hang in the balance, and he needed to understand the probable course of action of an unknown and unpredictable enemy.

"My Chief, I have been seeking guidance for many days now, with our ancestors and through the path of the stars. The answers I sought have not materialised as I expected." Nani paused to let her spoken words be absorbed and for effect. Chief raised his eyebrows at her in expectation.

"It was not to me that the spirits spoke to this time, Tane came to Marama. Chief, she's a girl with no experience of combat, battles or war. Still, when she opens her mouth, it is as if Tane is discussing strategy with her for his vengeance. I know it's unusual for a warrior to seek vengeance this way, but they were very close; she is my granddaughter. It seems she carries my gift."

Nani related the thoughts Marama had shared with her the previous night, making the Chief frown thoughtfully. Those were not topics a young woman commonly thought of, but they resonated with Tane's philosophy. However, he'd seen the girl wielding a stick on the beach with a skill he wished his taiaha (striking weapon) trainees possessed when she thought nobody was watching.

Perhaps the thoughts were both hers and Tane's combined. Did it really matter, he wondered? He needed to
devise a plan; to date, he'd been frustratingly unsuccessful at settling on anything.

"That cut from the battle seems to be slow healing to
my old eyes, Chief. Please come to my whare tomorrow
night, and my granddaughter will attend to it."

Nani rose smoothly from her perch on a log and
melted into the dark as silently as she had come. The
Chief admired her subtle manipulation to allow him to
speak with Tane through her granddaughter in the guise
of tending a wound.

He had nothing to lose, and he was curious. Many
of the thoughts Nani shared were chasing around in his
head, and maybe the chance to articulate them with
others might help him formulate a plan.

In Nani's whare, the Chief smelled the aroma of his
favourite herbs. Even though he had decided to come
here only a few moments ago, a cup awaited him. He believed he'd approached quietly, but perhaps his hearing
was no longer so sharp. Or maybe the old woman knew
he was coming.

He sat comfortably across from Nani and Marama,
who poked the fire to warm the herbal drink. The Chief
sipped from his bowl and raised his eyebrows. It was
his favourite brew, but there was an underlying tangy
flavour.

"Marama made the drink tonight and hoped to improve the taste and warming effects for my old bones and muscles. We hope it's to your liking."

The Chief knew that the drink's benefits were also for him. Nani was too polite to imply he needed them. He nodded his thanks to Marama, and her cheeks coloured in a shy blush, and she looked down. Not, however, before the Chief observed, his thanks had pleased her. Marama takes pride in her work, he thought but shows humility and respect for her elders. Even though she has shared in Tane's mischief, Nani has done well with her upbringing.

Marama looked up, startled when the Chief addressed her directly. The Chief was surprised by the unusual colour of her eyes in the firelight. They were the colour of the mountain pools, reflecting the green of new foliage and flickered like water in the shifting light. He had not taken much notice of her since she was a child; she was merely a shadow trailing after Nani or Tane. He observed her closely. There was strength in her angular features, and intelligence shone in her unusual eyes, but also a slight wariness. While she was not afraid of him, she was cautious.

"Your Nani tells me I should let you tend the cut on my arm from the battle. It heals more slowly than it should."

The change in her demeanour was immediate. This was ground she was clearly confident on. Marama was beside him in a heartbeat; he barely felt the air stir, and she was already examining his wound. She brought a light closer to see better, making noises before fetching a bowl of steaming water and herbs.

"I would like to cleanse the wound thoroughly with hot water and use herbs against infection to see inside the wound better; it may hurt a bit."

The Chief nodded his acquiescence, although she hadn't asked his permission, merely giving him a chance to object. She was confident and assumptive. He hoped she was competent as well.

While it was an excuse to visit, he also admitted that his arm was stiff and painful. Marama went about her business efficiently and cleansed the wound, frowning as she removed the dried blood. She probed around the outside of the scab, asking if it hurt more in this place or that.

"There's something inside the wound. It's festering and making poison inside, so the skin around it feels hot and tender. I need to reopen the wound to get it out."

The Chief nodded again for her to proceed.

"Nani, I need the obsidian needle knife, the pincers, something to absorb the blood and bind the wound. Can you assist me by holding the light?"

Nani brought the tools Marama asked for and held the light. Marama swiftly made the incision, opening the wound and allowing pus to run out. She swabbed rapidly and saw a sliver of wood. As the pus drained, blood seeped into the hole. She let the blood flow, feeling again, noticing the pressure was relieved. The wound was swabbed again; this time, it was red blood she wiped away. Marama took up the pincers, gripped the head of the wood sliver and pulled. It did not budge. She frowned, swabbed and looked more closely.

"The splinter is larger than I thought. I need a better grip and to push the flesh away to pull it out. It will hurt a lot."

Before she finished the words, she had levered the splinter away from the side of the wound, gripped the head in strong fingertips, and yanked the shard out.

The Chief did not cry out. He was covered in tā moko (cultural tattoo), had received many injuries, and was used to pain. His arm was sore, but it was a sharp pain, the kind he was accustomed to in battle. Marama bathed it again before smearing the hole with one of Nani's healing pastes and binding the arm.

"I must change it in the morning and make sure it starts healing."

Marama handed the Chief the wood splinter so he could examine the cause of his pain. The Chief was pleased the wood was removed. He had seen many warriors die from injuries that should not have killed them, often in the most painful circumstances.

"Thank you, Marama. Such an insignificant object is easily missed when it doesn't seem serious. You have learned many skills from Nani. Your mother would have been proud of you."

Marama looked at the Chief; he always seemed so distant and important. When she thought about it, she realised he was fair and kind. He gave praise where praise was due, as he'd done when they buried Tane with an elaborate warrior ceremony and when he'd chosen to honour Piki as a man with tā moko telling of the battle.

The Chief was a friend and confidant to Nani, and they often conferred on village matters. It warmed Marama to hear him acknowledge her mother would have been proud of her. She held the memories of her parents, their love, their embraces, shared laughter and home fiercely to her to stop them fading.

Marama smiled at the Chief, basking in his praise and daring to look into his eyes. She saw warmth, strength, confidence, and intelligence there. He definitely made her feel safer. As they exchanged looks, they found more in common than either supposed. The most unlikely kindred spirits.

Nani was satisfied. The meeting had gone better than planned. Marama was brewing another drink, this time with something to dull the pain.

The Chief watched the girl go about her work and chatted with Nani. They drank companionably around the fire, comfortable with each other.

"Marama, what thoughts do you and Tane have on the return of our enemy?"

There it was, the opening of the conversation they all wanted. Delivered smoothly, concisely and inclusive of a dead man and a girl without battle experience. Nani admired their Chief and his leadership. If she'd been born later, she'd have pursued him diligently. She chastised herself for being an old romantic fool instead of focusing on the problem.

"We believe that we must be vigilant. The exact timing of the invaders' return is a mystery. There are only a few places to land on the island with a force, and the tide needs to be favourable. You know all of this. If we post lookouts and learn of their approach, perhaps we can parley and save our village from bloodshed. Tane is our lookout; I'm confident he will warn us of their return. He desires vengeance for … for our lost future."

Marama looked away, shy, sharing her and Tane's hopes and dreams with Nani and the Chief. She regathered her composure and continued.

"Again, our wits will be our greatest ally. Tane is sure they will return with an even larger force than last time. While Mako burns to prove himself and take revenge, he cannot afford another costly failure. It could jeopardise his ambitions. He also vowed to return for me. He will desire a prize, a tangible symbol of his victory, and unfortunately, I'm a unique curiosity."

Nani gasped in horror.

"This is the plan you and Tane came up with? To use you as bait?" Nani paled as the blood drained from her face.

"Not bait, Nani," Marama looked squarely at the Chief, not her worried-looking Nani, "as a weapon. We need to use our collective cunning and knowledge to succeed."

And so the planning began in earnest. Options were discussed and debated as the stars wheeled overhead.

Eventually, Nani and Marama urged the Chief to rest and allow the healing potions to do their work so they could talk again in the morning when he came to change his dressing.

Moons waxed and waned without incident. People became concerned with the length of time the Chief's wound was taking to heal. They removed the bandage to reveal the cleanly healed skin to prevent further speculation or gossip. Instead, the Chief and Nani began planning a ceremony to honour the ancestors for their victory.

The villagers were busy preparing food and creating offerings of art, weaving and carving. They thought nothing of the time-consuming efforts of their Chief and spiritual guide, who were attending to essential matters.

Marama performed her usual duties and prepared meals with the Chief's head woman. In the evening, however, she attended the Chief and Nani in creating spiritual offerings and consulting the stars and moon. This was how the three conspirators planned for the most likely scenarios.

The village remained on high alert, with lookouts posted in shifts and pairs to ensure nobody fell asleep and left them at the mercy of a surprise attack.

All families were affected by the warriors lost or wounded in the battle, so there was no quibbling, just a quiet commitment to vigilance. The women lay awake with their children nestled against them while their men watched. They worried in the dark about the possibility of a further attack, but when morning came, they put on a brave face and worked hard to please their ancestors.

The ceremony began two days before the full moon. There were prayers and the burning of sacred offerings in a ceremonial fire at sunrise.

Nani summoned their ancestors to feast beside them and be revered with gifts to honour them for their protection. The Chief was bathed in the lagoon and cleansed of any lingering spirits the enemy may have brought to their island. His warriors and anyone who participated in the battle were also cleansed and anointed with ceremonial oil, making their bodies gleam as the sun spread its arms across the horizon in a fiery embrace.

Villagers felt uplifted and hopeful. The women laid their gifts in a miniature canoe with tears in their eyes as they thought of their departed loved ones.

The ceremony was followed by singing and dancing and an enormous feast. People ate in two sittings so the lookouts would have company, friends, and family to feast with. It was a day of healing, a balm for everyone with no work planned. Time was given to remember their ancestors and enjoy whanau (family) life together.

The following day, the Chief led his warriors in a rousing haka (warrior dance) to greet the rising sun. They exalted their ancestors until the sweat ran down their faces. Their bodies were pink and red with effort, and breath came fast and hard from the exertion. When the sun was up, they plunged into the water to rid themselves of salty sweat. The women in their families dried, oiled them and placed wreaths of flowers upon their heads or around their necks.

Men made offerings to the ancestors, placing them in the miniature canoe beside the women's. People came together again to share food from the umu (oven pit in the ground) that had been slowly cooking food since the prior evening.

Again, they ate in two groups, the delicious, steaming food savoured together, symbolic of their lives, constantly intertwined through time. There was laughter, fun, and an energetic and competitive dance contest.

Youths, not yet mated, vied for attention by showcasing their skills in flirtation. At the same time, some of the older villagers, who were the most talented dancers, competed energetically for the prizes.

It was a wonderful day that ended with games for the children, running and throwing contests. Everyone had practised since the festivities were announced. It was wise to practice if they had to run for their lives. The children searched in the sand for buried treasures they could keep to commemorate the day. Their families shouted encouragement and tried to point them to the places they thought they might find a prize. The villager's faces shone with love and pleasure in life.

Marama looked fondly at her Nani and their Chief, acknowledging their wisdom and ability to give people what they needed at the right time. One day, she hoped to guide a family, or maybe a village, with the skill and care of her co-conspirators. This evening, the three would play a more sombre role in thanking the ancestors and Gods for their mercy and imploring them to continue to do so.

The day passed amicably, with everyone well-fed and in a good mood. Even Piki admitted he could not eat any more for a couple of hours after the feast. And he danced enthusiastically as well. The smooth dance moves of such a chubby boy never ceased to amuse people. Everyone cheered when he flirted with the mated women, including the Chief's women, and then with Nani.

Nani played along and surprised the villagers with a few dance moves to rival Piki's. This caused a general uproar of whistling and clapping and resulted in Nani awarding a very pleased Piki a coveted prize.

The moon rose, pregnant with light. Nani deemed the evening the most auspicious to commune with the Gods and ancestors. It was one night before the moon was full. The Chief, Nani and Marama crouched in the dark before the receding tide. The ocean was a blanket of silver behind them. The theatre of the evening was not lost on Marama. It added to the spirituality and awe. Nani began her call. First to the Gods of the ocean, forest, moon and sky, followed by the other Gods they relied on for survival.

No God was forgotten. The keepers of the spirits took great care not to offend any deity. Then Nani and the Chief called the ancestors together, reciting the names back to the founders of their tribe and island hundreds of years before.

The wind was behind them and carried their voices inland to where their people stood in their finest attire and adornments, bearing their best weapons or implements. They stood shoulder to shoulder quietly as serious this evening as they had been ebullient in the morning. The air thrummed with the presence of spirits, and the villagers collectively held their breath.

Facing the sea, Marama drew the stone box from beneath her cloak. It carried a glowing ember. She blew on it, adding tinder before lighting a slim reed. The Chief stood, Nani behind him, as he chanted to the Gods and ancestors to hear their prayers for protection against the coming storm.

On cue, Marama touched the burning reed to the apex of the channels they'd dug before everyone arrived. The mixture of herbs and minerals glowed on either side of the Chief and Nani in time with their progress up the beach. A fiery glow, eerie smoke and a pungent herbal aroma filled the air. Gasps told Marama the effect was better than they'd hoped. They had never seen anything like this before. In secret, it took much trial and error to create the slow-burning effect for this evening. It was worth it. Marama moved from side to side, waving palm fronds behind the Chief and Nani to distribute the offerings in the sand. The wind scattered the remaining traces on the beach to await the incoming tide.

The sound of the sea swirled in Marama's head like listening to shells. The tide was running out, but a huge wave crashed on the beach and chased behind Marama, foaming around her ankles. This was not planned. Marama swooned and pitched forward in the sand.

"I will help you", the wave hissed on the sand.

"Be brave, namesake" whispered the moon.

"He is coming. You must be ready," breathed Tane.

Marama sat upright, eyes wide - glowing green. Nani was by her side, singing thanks to the ancestors for coming in their time of need.

"The sea will help us and the moon. We must be ready. They are coming," Marama told Nani and the Chief.

They both nodded sagely, and the Chief turned to address his people.

"Our prayers have been answered. Tangaroa, the God of the sea himself, sent his voice to this beach to offer us help. The moon lends us her bravery, and Tane comes in spirit to Marama. He warns us that our enemy is approaching. We are fortunate to have such auspicious words shared with all of us. What is more, we are ready."

The Chief turned to Nani, who handed him an ornate cloak she had made. It was woven with intricate symbols and patterns. Feathers and hundreds of tiny pieces of shell adorned it. The cloak shimmered in the moonlight with a celestial beauty. The Chief turned to Marama and placed it around her shoulders.

"I welcome you to your role as a spirit guide to our village, Marama. Has ever one village been so blessed with two healers and two spiritual guides? With this token, we honour the Gods and Ancestors who have given us a bounty of gifts and chosen to speak with us through you."

Marama knelt before their Chief, and he kissed her forehead, accepting her offer of service.

"The spirits have revealed a way to victory through Nani and Marama. We have much to do. Rest well this night, for our wits need only to be as sharp as our weapons, and we will prevail. With the Gods and our ancestors on our side, the enemy will find that increasing the number of warriors will not help them."

A feast was laid out in the carved ceremonial canoe, along with the offerings of the last two days from the men, women and children. The Chief and three of his most trusted warriors shouldered the canoe and carried it into the water. Nani followed behind, chanting prayers to the Gods. The Chief and his warriors placed the canoe in the water, and Nani used her ember box to set the canoe alight.

The inside of the canoe was coated in animal fat and oil. Flames licked and flickered. The Chief waded into the surf, chanting his prayers and launching the canoe, laden with gifts, into the arms of the outgoing tide. The villagers lit the flaming torches on the beach so the ancestors and Gods could see them in their finery and know they had been honoured by all.

Silvered water lit the passage of the gifts as they travelled through the channel and beyond the reef. The villagers sang together of their ancestor's voyage to the island and the voyage of their offerings to the ancestors and the Gods. They held hands in a display of unity and ended the evening sharing a specially brewed ceremonial drink.

Nani and Marama each filled coconut bowls and handed them to their Chief, who invited every person to take a draught. The drink was fermented over time and affected everyone differently. Children often became sleepy, allowing their mothers to participate in the dancing that followed.

Drummers struck up a fast beat, and the final festivities began with dancing. They celebrated into the night while the children drowsed, wrapped in cloaks on the edge of the firelight. Young lovers stole away to share embraces in the dark. Marama felt a stab of pain as she saw a couple sneaking off. She swiped tears from her eyes.

"I am in your heart, my love, always." She sensed rather than heard Tane's words of comfort. Marama pulled her cloak closer, hugging her arms around her knees and wishing they were Tane's arms instead. Nevertheless, she felt a rush of warmth as she always did when Tane came to her. Aided no doubt by the potent brew that she had helped to make.

When Piki, grinning like an idiot, wiggled his way over to claim the newest spirit guide for a dance, Marama threw off her melancholy with a giggle and joined him in his crazy dance.

Lightheaded and carefree, Marama submitted herself to the intoxicating call, abandoning thoughts of revenge and planning. For once, to live in the moment.

The following day, the Chief summoned his warriors. The people were due to meet in the evening, and there was a heightened sense of urgency and anticipation. The women bustled around to finish all their chores early, and the children were also sent on numerous errands. Everyone was curious about what they would do when the enemy returned. Still, they were so busy that they hardly had time to speculate or gossip.

They were not scared. They'd all been on the beach last night and had felt and seen the power of the spirits. They had heard the prophecy and seen the signs and felt protected, not only by the Gods and Ancestors but by the connection of their Chief and the spirit guides to them. The confidence and calm of the Chief reassured them that they could survive the invasion. What hope did an enemy have when the dead were on their side? The villagers listened attentively to the plan that the Chief outlined. The warriors were briefed in the morning, so they were less surprised than when the information was first revealed. Eyes widened, eyebrows raised, furtive glances cast. However, as the Chief, Nani, and Marama sat still as stones, the villagers began to nod in under-standing. This was not the kind of plan that any of them had expected. If it worked, however, many lives could be saved, which was not a consideration to be taken lightly.

Many preparations had been made in the guise of particular tasks allocated by the Chief or Nani in the preceding weeks. The villagers now understood what the Chief meant when he told them they were ready, and they were much comforted by this thought.

Marama felt the whispering inside her head, pulling at the fog covering her brain. She sat bolt upright in bed.

"He is here, Marama, so close now."

I am ready, my love. The thought was spoken to Tane.

"It is time now," Nani said. Not a question, just a statement, and Nani was seated wide awake beside the fire, already preparing what was needed. Nani went straight to the Chief, then awakened her helpers.

The Chief was standing with his warriors in battle garb when the lookout scout arrived. The scout was surprised to be greeted by a dark, silent, bustling village.

"How long," asked the Chief, "until they make the beach?"

"They track past the outer reef moving swiftly south and are positioning to come through the southern channel as the tide turns. They will be behind the village with the dark clouds and the small mountain shielding them from our view and dampening the noise of the landing. They are mostly in darkness, more than one canoe. It was only by the will of the Gods and ancestors that I saw them outlined briefly as they were navigating the reef. We have time but need to hurry," he said as he dropped, puffing to his knees.

The Chief patted his shoulders. He had sprinted to give them the news of the approach and was utterly spent.

Everyone moved to their allocated positions purposefully, as they had practised many times before. Then they waited.

Chapter 3

The first canoe landed on the beach. The forty warriors jumped smoothly into the surf. They assisted the tide, pushing the canoe onto the sand as the waters receded behind them.

They assumed an arrowhead protective fighting formation as the second canoe arrived with forty more fighters. Their leader, Mako, sat stony-faced in the prow. They scouted the fringes of the beach to check they'd not been seen, and an ambush didn't await them.

Satisfied that no large force surrounded the cove, they grouped around their leader. As they turned to the path, a burning circle of light appeared before a boulder on their western flank.

In the middle of the flaming circle stood the green-eyed maiden Mako came to claim. Smoke drifted around her. She lit two torches crossed against her chest from the flames and planted them on either side.

The warriors gaped at the vision before them. It must be a Goddess or a spirit. They'd never seen or experienced anything like it.

The scouts had thoroughly checked the beach, but there she was. It was as if she'd emerged from the ground. They rubbed their eyes to ensure they were awake and tried not to appear afraid, though the fine hairs on their bodies prickled when the men realised they were not imagining her.

Marama stood tall. Her eyes were outlined with paste made from soot and glowed jewel-like in the firelight, shimmering and watery from the smoke. Marama's hair was combed into a cloud. A red-gold halo in the firelight. Mother-of-pearl combs held the hair from her face. Lips were stained and oiled in a sultry pout. The shell cloak the Chief had placed around her shoulders, made with love and care by Nani, draped around her shoulders. It shimmered eerily in the guttering torchlight.

The women had adorned her with polished coconuts covering her breasts and a skirt made of fresh leaves around her slim hips. The attire accentuated her shape and provided curves on a lean, muscular body. Shadows on her skin enhanced Marama's shapeliness as much as possible, and the effect was pleasing.

A shark tooth necklace hung around her neck, and an enormous pearl dripped at the end. The pearl belonged to the Chief's head woman. It had been a betrothal gift. The woman's father was the wealthy chief of the largest settlement on the island.

She'd offered it to Marama, hoping it might help save the lives of her three children. Arms were decorated with mother-of-pearl, carved wooden bracelets and armbands. Her healing bag dangled from her skirt. Feet and legs were wrapped with pliant shark skin decorated with shells and coral. They had decided against any tattooing except her healer's mark. Letting the richness of attire and status as a healer announce her importance and rank. Many treasures had flowed from the whare of the villagers. They knew Marama risked losing her home and possibly her life to save them.

Marama began her chant to the Gods and ancestors in full voice. Nani drilled her unstintingly, making her sing into the wind while walking in the soft sand on the beach and when running to the waterfall to fetch water.

Then, Marama began the dance they had choreographed. Telling the story of how she met Mako. They were unsure if they could communicate in the same language, so the visual dance included many hand gestures. Marama noticed she could understand the few exchanges between the warriors and breathed an inward sigh of relief that communication would be simple. As she re-enacted her emergence from the lagoon, she looked straight at him as she had that day. It was a hot, burning look, filled with desire.

'A man sees what he wants to see,' Nani advised her. Nani was right. Mako saw a passion that mirrored his desire to possess her, while Marama was driven by revenge.

"You are doing well, my love. I am smitten again, and I feel your anger, which is also mine," Tane whispered.

Marama clung to Tane's encouragement.

The next part of the plan was tenuous. It relied on the vision and Marama's powers of persuasion. At the end of the dance, Marama dropped to her knees.

"The Gods have revealed to me, the spirit guide, that I am your woman." Marama paused for effect as she'd seen the Chief and Nani do when commanding an audience. She noticed numerous reactions from the men. Surprise, fear, envy, relief, and Mako's face wore wariness and lust. They all revered the Gods and the spirits, but this wasn't a man easily influenced and who was used to taking what he wanted.

"Haere mai, haere mai, haere mai (come, come)," Marama chanted and gestured with her hands and arms as if she pulled on an invisible rope.

A ceremonial canoe beached as her ritual and song ended. The men examined the canoe. Scanning the dark water for signs of other vessels. There was only the tiny canoe, beautifully carved and laden with wealth.

The warriors whispered and gaped at Marama with wonder in their eyes. Their leader motioned them to silence, and they obeyed. He did not want their superstitions to cloud his judgment in this encounter. Their lives might depend on it. He felt he was being bewitched; he wanted the girl more than ever, but his survival instincts were jangling a warning.

"I am to leave this island with you so it is ordained by the Gods, and I have awaited your return to fulfil the promise and a prophecy. I cannot go with you unless you forfeit your revenge on the village. I was promised to another."

Marama looked into Mako's eyes. This time in supplication, pleading for him to take her. It had been difficult for her to learn, and Marama hoped she'd made the correct expression. She had practised with her face over the pool in the creek.

"If you take me by force, raise my home and kill my family, I will be dishonoured. Worthless, my ancestors and spirit guides will abandon me, and our union will be short. If you forfeit utu (vengeance), the warriors of my village also lose their right to revenge on you. The gifts in the waka (canoe) are yours as my mate offering from my father, and he'll also compensate the family of my betrothed with similar riches. Should you take all by force, I will die, and a blood feud with my people and father will begin. My family does not want me to go. They obey the will of the Gods who foretold my departure at birth. Our life together, the children we will have, won't exist."

Marama looked up with tears, and the emotion was raw and powerful. As she spoke aloud, she thought of Tane, their lost future and the children they should have shared. These words affected Mako. He believed Marama had seen a vision of their children. Leaders want many sons, and if gifts like these were offered, maybe daughters too. The girl was young but already a healer and spirit guide, a valuable prize.

Mako was thoughtful and motioned the three men in his inner circle to his side. They moved away from Marama and the men to discuss strategy.

"What do you think of this?" Mako asked.

"I think we should tie her up, gag her, attack the village and take our revenge. Steal the wealth offered, plunder the village, and paddle home fast. Or we could kill her. I doubt she can be trusted," said Mako's brother. He nodded and weighed his brother's words carefully. If this raid failed, or he was killed in battle by that wily old Chief, his brother would become chief instead of him. Should his brother survive a successful raid, he would claim the girl, plunder, gifts and glory. The opinion may have been forthright, that they stick to their plan, or it could be coloured by his brother's ambition. There was no love between them. They had always been rivals. Mako looked to his best friend since childhood next. He was a brave, skilled warrior who loved a good fight and possessed an excellent strategic mind.

"There is some merit in the parley. I enjoy battle and returning home with a canoe full of plunder, but they already know we're here. If they foresaw our arrival, we also don't know if they've summoned other villages to assist with defence. The risks have increased. There is also merit in returning home with the prize you came for. The girl is unique, wealthy and skilled. All your warriors return without injury or loss and a horde of treasure. Last time, we underestimated our enemy, and the battle did not go as planned. I would like to paddle home with a victory this time. What does your experience tell you, Starman?"

Mako noted his friend cautioned him regarding returning home in defeat again, and he wanted to know their navigator's opinion. The most experienced man in the canoe, Starman navigated by the heavens as his ancestors had done for hundreds of years. He'd been on every raid with Mako's father since he was a small boy. This man deserved respect. He possessed experience, bravery, caution, and spirituality. He was diplomatically impartial in the leadership rivalry between Mako and his brother - an impossible position.

"Good, but opposing arguments from both of your counsellors," said Starman. "I think carefully about what, if anything, I can add to the discussion. I feel bewitched by the girl as I don't know how she came here or how she has created the magic around her - other than through the spirit world. Her name is Marama, the same name as the moon. Is she a moon Goddess? When she recited her whakapapa (ancestral genealogy) in her chant, she did not name her father. Only referred to him as her father from the sea. Perhaps her father is a God of or the God of the sea. She looks so different from anyone I have ever met on all my journeys. I am a superstitious mariner who does not wish to offend any God of the sea. My craft relies on their benevolence. I ask myself, who can afford such riches as we are offered - twice? I also ask myself if we want to bring a blood feud from such a father to our home - even if we are successful. The warrior's heart yearns for battle, and I have seen many. On this occasion, I have misgivings on both courses of action for logical and spiritual reasons. The decision is yours, Mako. I would happily paddle home without battle, girl or gifts, offending nobody. Perhaps I'm becoming cautious with age."

Starman looked thoughtfully at the young leader and did not envy him this decision. He had deliberately left a middle path open by being so cautious. His words were truthful; Starman knew he could die on this island. Their men were all spooked by the strangeness of the evening.

Mako nodded his thanks to his men. The decision was his, and he appreciated the different perspectives provided by each man. The words weighed carefully before being spoken. His navigator's caution resonated with his own sense of unease. He must put aside his need to claim the prize and consider the options with a clear mind and sound logic. This raid could determine his future as the next chief of his people and, therefore, the preeminent leader of their island nation as his father was now. His fate and life were pivoting on this decision.

The surprise, the spirituality of the lone girl's greeting and parley conditions again threw their plans into disarray. The spirit world is not my domain, he thought wryly. Mako didn't believe dead people influenced lives. The battle was where he shone, but how else had the girl appeared in the exact landing spot? Where had the gifts come from, he pondered.

Contemplating these questions meant his men, many superstitious, were unsettled and unpredictable. Two of his advisors wanted to go home without loss of life, which translated to two-thirds of the men feeling the same. Mako needed to return home in triumph. He could not fail again.

"I need to commune with our ancestors on this matter," he announced. "Only our old ones can determine our path. They promised her to me, but the matter of forfeiting utu is not a decision I take lightly. I must take time to consult our tīpuna for guidance."

Mako took a position opposite Marama and made his supplication to his ancestors, giving him time to think and weigh his options.

Marama wished fervently he communed with his ancestors quickly before the torches burnt out. She knew he would decide either way before the tide turned. It was only a few minutes before he announced that his ancestors had chosen her as his mate long ago. However, they demanded that the Chief give the forfeit of vengeance as an oath. The moon child Goddess could not speak for the warriors of the tribe. By naming the girl a child of the moon and a Goddess, he was raising her status and adding to his when she became his woman.

Marama thanked the Chief and Nani for cunning and wily planning. They had organised signals to summon the Chief, Nani, both of them or all of the warriors. She raised a shell to her lips with her left hand and raised her right hand into the air. A conch call reverberated around the beach when she blew into her tiny shell. Piki's little brother was positioned in a tree on the hill overlooking the beach to see Marama's signals. The rocky cleft sent echoes from the conch shell bouncing backwards and forwards, so it sounded like it came from many directions. It was an illusion, but the enemy was already on edge. The summons was another strange occurrence in a night dominated by Gods and spirits.

Marama closed her eyes and counted in her head until she knew the Chief would be in position on the rock ledge above. It was a dangerous moment for them. Their Chief would be as alone and exposed as she was. Marama threw both arms into the air, dramatically widening her eyes as flames appeared on the rock above, dancing light on the Chief. The Chief was oiled and unarmed, standing still and stoic. She raised her hands in supplication.

"My Chief, you must make an oath to the Gods. Forfeit the right to utu upon these people. Their ancestors demanded this as ours foretold my destiny," said Marama.

The Chief cut a commanding figure alone on the rock. He looked down upon Marama.

"Aue! That this prophecy should come to pass in my days. Your father has made peace with your betrothed and his family. My heart quails at making the oath that the Gods demand. Our village laments the loss of our spirit guide and healer. I am only a Chief and a man. It is not my place to question destiny set by the Gods or the spirits," he said, spitting the words like sour bile from his mouth.

The Chief bowed his head, pausing momentarily as the warriors on the beach waited on his words.

"Hear this, invaders, I pledge an oath that if you forfeit your right to utu and leave these shores peacefully, with our moon daughter and her wealth, I and all the warriors of our village relinquish the right to avenge our fallen."

Mako's eyes were daggers hurled at the man who thwarted his initial raid and disrupted the second.

"Do you think me a witless fool? Old man. You may have summoned reinforcements. I demand your oath includes all the men on the island, not just your village."

The Chief's jawline tightened, and his eyes glittered. Obsidian chips of fury. Pleased with his cunning, Mako placed his hands on his hips in impatient bravado. His men muttered among themselves. None of them had thought of the other villages.

His voice stone, the Chief repeated the oath - all the men of the island forfeit vengeance. The flames extinguished, and the Chief vanished with the smoke that drifted in the air.

The leader turned to his men.

"The oath was taken as our ancestors wanted. I, in turn, forfeit the right to revenge in exchange for the moon Goddess and her betrothal gifts. We all need battle and revenge, but we are only men, flesh and blood. This has been a night of prophecy, spirits and Gods, and we dare not offend them by refusing proffered gifts. As your leader, I would take you all home wealthy and unharmed to your families without incurring a blood feud that may last hundreds of years. Split the gifts evenly between the waka and Starman, make an offering in the ceremonial canoe with prayers for a safe journey home. We will launch it on the outgoing tide when we leave."

The warriors collectively breathed a sigh of relief. Their battle lust had deserted them during the night, and they were glad to be turning their canoes toward home.

Their leader strode towards the strange Goddess. The circle had disappeared, and she stood in the light of the guttering torches, green eyes glittering.

He held out his hand to her, and she placed her golden hand in his. He was relieved her hand was warm and human with a firm grip. They regarded each other, and the corners of her mouth lifted in a victorious smile.

So she had wanted him to claim her. He wondered what she'd seen in their future that made her determined to leave home and follow a prophecy. He drew her cloak around her shoulders and pulled her possessively toward him, even though shells scratched his skin. She was lithe, but her body was healthy and firm. She would bear him many children.

He was captivated by the colour of her eyes and had never wanted anything more than he wanted her. The thought shocked him. He was not an emotional man, and he'd had and discarded his fair share of women. But he'd never been drawn to anyone as he was to her. Mako shook his head to clear his thoughts and led Marama to his canoe. Seated her in the middle next to him, where he could get to know her on their journey home. He claimed her before his men as his prize.

Nani stood atop a cliff in the dark, the foliage behind, hiding her silhouette as she watched the scene unfold. Her heart beat rapidly, and she implored her ancestors and Tane to protect Marama from harm. The plan was daring and risky. The invaders landed in one of the better locations to create drama. Marama was hidden inside a space hollowed in the rock by the sea, the entrance concealed by seaweed. Her appearance on the beach, out of nowhere, unsettled the enemy. Many variables could have, and could still, go wrong. Ultimately, logic, spiritual fear and valuable plunder had won over the enemy to a peaceful resolution. Nani watched her precious granddaughter climb into the waka of their enemy with the poise and grace of an actual Goddess. Her pride warmed the fear residing in old bones. It was not yet over.

The Chief watched from his vantage point above the rock platform.

Marama had played her part well; there was definitely something otherworldly about her tonight, and there was no doubting her bravery and selflessness. She had also read the enemy's thoughts and motivations despite her limited experience. Even with her strange appearance, the moon daughter would make a formidable woman for a leader.

The situation was now out of his hands and in the lap of the Gods and the ancestors. He had taken an oath that could not be broken. The Chief was tense. There would be no release of his tension in battle this time, and worry gnawed like a ravenous rodent. As the Chief, he was unaccustomed to the lack of involvement or control at this stage of engagement. The burden of decisions and actions sat on the bony shoulders of a fearless young woman. All he could do was call on the ancestors and Gods to protect her. Instead, he placed the spiritual cloak he wore into battle around her.

Marama sat forward, peering toward the channel as the waka launched. Her namesake shone, and she offered silent thanks that the parley went well and she was still alive. She didn't look back at the beach, the island and her home becoming smaller. Marama could feel the gaze of Nani and her Chief on her back, and she was comforted by their spiritual presence. Mako pulled her close. Marama held his gaze and snuggled closer into his body as if she were cold. In truth, Marama was feverish. Tightly bottled rage an internal inferno. Instead, she smiled gently, hoping it was filled with promise and he would again see what he wanted to see. The plan was in motion, the bait taken; the rest was up to the Gods.

Mako relaxed as the canoes pulled away from the shore. He longed to be at sea and paddling home. His father would be pleased with the outcome of the raid. The gifts, the girl, returning with all his men and a story that legends were made of should be enough to secure his position. He was relaxed and drained after the mentally challenging evening. Mako determined he must spend more time on spiritual training when he got home.

Perhaps his new woman could guide him. She exuded an ethereal presence and could commune with the spirits. He pulled her closer to reassure himself she was there. As she cuddled closer to him for warmth or comfort, he felt fiercely protective of her. When she looked up at him and smiled, he longed to be home and alone with her. It was a strange feeling. There was a slight tingling in his body; he'd never had much faith in the stories of love that abounded in history and legend. Maybe this was how it felt. He shook his head again to clear his mind and stay awake. They were approaching the channel to the outer reef.

Marama felt Mako's body slouch against her.

He was tough. The cone snail venom took its time working. Nani taught her how to extract the poison, and they'd devised several ways of administering it, including coating some of the sharper shells on her cloak. The most significant risk was that she could scratch herself if careless. She didn't have to pierce his skin with the implement she carried in her medicine bag, which would have alerted him and cost Marama her life. Still, she had been prepared to do that for Tane.

They were approaching the narrow part of the channel. She shifted her body from supporting Mako. He fell backwards with a thump.

Marama screamed a high-pitched squeal that could have woken the dead.

"My love, my love, don't leave me. Aue!" she cried. It was a passionate cry to Tane but sewed panic in the canoe.

The men rushed to their leader's side, pushing Marama out of the way and calling the other canoe to stop.

Marama stumbled, falling on the hoard of gifts and grabbed a tiny, exquisite, covered bowl decorated with coral. Inside the top was rendered fat, and in the separated bottom was a glowing coal. She released it from its prison. Treasures were covered, or sitting on, beds of fat and oil or packed in dried grasses. The touch of the ember created a whoosh of flames in the canoe, adding to the panic. The first canoe paddled frantically against the tide that had just turned to aid Mako.

Marama went overboard with a scream, grabbing a gourd as she did. The cloak became heavy as it was soaked with water and carefully weighted with stones sewn into the bottom hem. She sank slowly, even with the gourd.

Mako's best friend hurled his spear at her. The water slowed it, and the outgoing tide pulled it off course. Marama sank into the depths, her glittering cloak attracting curious reef fish as she went.

As the second canoe pulled back toward the burning wreck of their leader, they came close to the rocks. Fiery balls were launched at them by the women and children. Those with the best throwing arms.

One of the flaming projectiles hit the gifts, and the second canoe erupted in flames. The warriors in both canoes scrambled to pull water on board to douse the fire, but the women and children threw vessels filled with fats and oils to feed the flames. They had filled half coconut shells, sealed them with resin and bound them together, but they split as they hit the deck. Their contents splattered everywhere, including onto the men, providing more fuel for the hungry fire. Warriors hurled their spears at the rocks, but they clattered harmlessly as the throwing team took shelter. Just as the men considered jumping into the sea, a freak wave lifted their waka and dashed them against the rocks. The burning oil covered and consumed many, but others were knocked unconscious and sank in the waves.

Mako was already crossing to his ancestors' realm as his peaceful slumber morphed into his body, shutting down. The warriors were all swimmers, but the outgoing tide in the channel pulled them out swiftly before dashing them against the rocks. Any who did manage to clamber out of the water scraped their bleeding limbs on the coral reef and were pelted with missiles by the women and children. Even the freak wave had been orchestrated by the women who heaved the final push that released a massive boulder on the side of the cliff into the sea. The village toiled tirelessly to loosen it, then secure it, and all prayed it would not fall too soon.

And so it was that the oath was not broken. None of the warriors of the village sought vengeance as promised. The women and children were not warriors and had not given their pledge to forfeit any retribution.

The mothers, aunts, cousins, younger brothers, sisters, nieces and nephews claimed the right to utu.

Under the waves, Marama was buffeted by violent currents pushing and pulling her body. She removed some of the stones from the bottom of the cloak, so she hung suspended in deep water and kicked out for the beach. She'd repeatedly swum this path in the channel and practised against the tide. It was a challenging swim. Marama clung to rocks to avoid the sucking waters whenever she could, using the cloak, turned inside out to protect her skin from the coral and the poisoned shells. Marama also took breaths from the small gourd, releasing the air slowly from her lungs as she went. Still, progress was slow, and Marama reckoned she'd need to surface long before she reached the shore.

"Thank you, my love," Tane whispered. "He is gone, and I am avenged. I will always be with you, but you must go on. You must live as you have much to do before joining us. I love you."

Marama felt Tane's arms around her and then the strong surge of a wave that catapulted her forward against the outgoing pull. It was the same wave that threw the canoes against the rocks. Marama saw a shadow above her. The ceremonial canoe they used to offer gifts to the sea. It should have been pulled out to sea in the tide, but it was catapulted forward by the freak wave as she had been. She rose slowly to the surface and climbed aboard, utterly spent but exultant that Tane was avenged. She lay flat in the canoe and paddled with her arms against the flow. Glancing up, she saw an outrigger surging toward her from the shore with the Chief and her worried Nani sitting in the prow. She allowed herself a smile before her eyes closed in complete exhaustion.

The villagers erupted in jubilant celebration.

Families laughed and cried together in a wave of relief, expelling the tension built over the many days of preparation. They knew the risk they were taking, especially Marama and their Chief. To avoid a battle, that win or lose would have decimated their village.

When the women and children torched the waka and the sea smashed the invaders' canoes on the rocks, the watching villagers dropped to their knees in fervent thanks to the Gods and their ancestors who provided them with inspiration and courage. They lived in a legend, participating in a story that would be told for many years. There was an outpouring of love and thanks for Marama as the outrigger plucked her from the receding tide and beached.

At first, they saw her limp body and thought she had made the ultimate sacrifice for them. But as the Chief scooped her in his arms to carry her ashore, they saw Nani throwing a dry cloak over the girl and rubbing her hands to warm her blood.

They also saw a body wash ashore clinging to a gourd, one of the gift offerings. The gourd was filled with fragrant dried flowers and floated away from the burning waka. The warrior had been thrown out of the canoe as it collided with the rocks, and the gourd appeared bobbing in the waves. He clung to it and kicked for the shore. His survival instincts drew every ounce of effort from his muscles, and the God of the Sea, whom he had worshipped all his life, took mercy on him. He was propelled to the beach by a huge wave.

The villagers surrounded him, spears at the ready, but the man did not move. They sent a runner to fetch their Chief and Nani, who were busy making Marama comfortable. The Chief's head woman undressed Marama with Nani before she snuggled in a makeshift bed, slowly warming her water-chilled body. She cradled Marama in her arms like a child, and tears ran down her cheeks. They were grateful tears. She could have lost her man, her three children and her home in one night. Instead, they were planning an impromptu feast with everyone together, and this fearless girl had played an enormous part in the outcome.

Marama was still sleeping, but her face was serene and content. She was so very young. The transference of body heat was taking place nicely. Marama's limbs began to suffuse with warmth, and the colour returned to her face. Still, the Chief's woman cuddled her close, wanting to protect and care for her as a mother would for as long as possible. It was the least she could do.

The Chief strode across the sand where the sole survivor from the invading canoes lay, surrounded by half a dozen armed warriors. Nani hurried along behind him as best she could. Her old bones were feeling the fatigue of the evening. She could not help herself; she clambered up the cliff for a better vantage point of events. Then she'd climbed down again in the dark. A spiritual link was not enough for her at the time. She wanted a physical line of sight of her granddaughter. To know what to ask for and to guide Tane.

Walking in the soft sand was tiring, and Nani was breathless as the Chief turned to her with raised brows.

"All the invading warriors perished except this man. It's an unusual outcome for a man to be thrown upon the shore when the tide is going out. Don't you think? He was their navigator, a man of the sea. What is your interpretation of this Nani? I feel he is favoured by the Gods."

The Chief looked to Nani for her counsel.

"You are right, my Chief; he has undoubtedly been saved for a reason.

We cannot offend the Gods by going against their wishes. Nani bent to examine the navigator. His pulse was good enough. Nani had his body turned on its side and cleared his airways. He vomited the seawater he had swallowed in the waves, coughing and spluttering, before closing his eyes again.

"Please take him to the village, and I will treat him. I must do my best for the God of the sea who saved all of us tonight."

Fatigue was forgotten as Nani hurried to check on Marama and gently kissed her cheek before scurrying back to the village.

Chapter 4

Marama's eyes flew open. She was in their whare, warm, dry and alive, she hoped. Nani smiled at her, a steaming bowl in her hand.

Her stomach growled, responding to the smell of food. The events of the evening flooded back. Their plans worked, Tane was avenged, and the village was saved. Outside, revelry was in full swing. Drums beat, and people sang and danced.

The aroma of delicious food floated in the air. Marama felt ravenous and elated; they had done it. She threw off the covers and grabbed Nani in a fierce embrace. Nani blinked away unwanted tears in triumphant eyes and used her free hand to hug Marama.

"Eat something, Marama. I can hear your puku complaining of neglect, and the people have left a feast at the door for you."

They sat by the fire together. Marama ate like she'd never eaten before. Everything was scrumptious. She didn't remember eating since Tane died. Marama knew she had but had no recollection of what or the taste. So grief-stricken at first, then focused on planning; all other tasks were mechanical. They grinned at each other as Marama wolfed down enormous quantities of food, licking her fingers and lips as she devoured one dish after another.

Piki would have been proud of her efforts. Still, she didn't stop until her once flat belly was swollen and distended from her efforts. An enormous belch warned there was no more space. Marama and Nani giggled like giddy teenagers, eyes streaming when the Chief popped in. His face split in a grin to see his co-conspirators in such fine form. Nani wiped tears from her eyes and pointed at the empty bowls, then Marama's huge belly. The Chief's eyebrows shot up at the sight of Marama's puku. When his woman poked her head through the door, she laughed.

"We shall name the baby mini Marama," she chortled before grabbing Marama for a hug.

"Come," said the Chief, "the whole village is waiting for you to join the celebration."

Marama looked down at her swollen belly and put her hand to her salt-encrusted hair, slightly panicked.

"Nobody will care what you look like, Marama. They are so proud of you they will only see the sun shining from your backside and smell frangipani flowers from your bottom," said Nani, rolling her eyes dramatically.

"Nani is right. To us, you are the most beautiful woman in the world, but," she turned to the Chief, "a young woman must feel beautiful as well. So give us five minutes to get ready."

The Chief nodded and left them to untangle Marama's hair and dress her.

Primped and scrubbed, Marama emerged from their whare amid the festivities.

When the people saw her, they cheered and called her name, lifting her onto the shoulders of the village warriors. They carried her to a raised seat next to the Chief, covered in garlands of flowers. The villagers touched Marama, murmuring their thanks for her bravery, averting the battle, saving their homes and children, and avenging their loved ones. Tears glittered in response to their emotions, but she smiled to convey her happiness.

The Chief placed her gently as the guest of honour between himself and Nani.

"There will be time for thanks and formal ceremonies in the coming days. We celebrate our victory tonight and honour the Gods, our ancestors and Marama." He raised his drink to Marama, and the celebration erupted with new vigour.

Nani slipped away to check on her patient. Marama was in good health and good hands, enjoying the evening. No doubt there would be sore heads from the celebrating and feet from dancing in the morning, so she would prepare remedies for both before bed.

First, she must attend to the navigator. He was close to drowning, but he was a healthy man. With the proper care, he would recover. A warrior watched over him. Nani nodded to him as she entered the guest whare. Poor young man, she thought, missing the feast. However, the Chief organised a roster so nobody sat with him long. As the older warriors retired, they would sleep in the guest hut with him as a precaution. He was the navigator of their enemy, and they needed to be vigilant.

Eventually, he would awaken, and he was now in their midst. Thoughts could turn immediately to vengeance or escape, and they couldn't allow either.

Nani knelt by his side. She listened to his heart and breathing, felt his skin, tended the bump on his head and the coral scrapes on his arms. The navigator was beautiful in repose. Angular planes, high cheekbones, and a straight nose. He certainly looked favoured by a God, tall and handsome. She finished bathing his cuts, and his eyelids fluttered. He opened his eyes. Nani's concerned gaze met him. His head felt fuzzy and throbbed with pain, eyelids heavy. The old woman fetched a steaming bowl that smelt of herbs. She held it to his lips. He hesitated. What if she was trying to poison him?

"If we wanted to kill you, we could have done so on the beach while you were unconscious. Now, try and sip this slowly. It will help with the pain." Nani put her arm under his head to let him tilt and sip without choking.

"The God of the sea decided to intervene in your fate. We owe him much, and I have sworn to use my spiritual and healing skills to bring you back to health. The Chief of the village and I are in accord and share a belief that you are favoured. You alone, of all the raiding party, have survived this night, which speaks to us of an unful-filled purpose in this world. Blink if you understand my words." He blinked in understanding.

"If you are well enough tomorrow, we will speak. I want to understand who you are and have a vague inkling of your purpose. But perhaps you can shed some light on that yourself. For now, you must rest. I have given you a healing brew that will dull the pain and take you into the deep sleep that will assist your body with repairing itself."

Nani barely finished speaking when the navigator slipped into the unconsciousness of assisted sleep. She patted the young man, guarding him on the shoulder.

"He will not awaken until late morning tomorrow. The Chief asks that you go and join the rest of the villagers. He has allocated the watch to some of the young war-riors in training. The guard duty will raise their mana and allow all his warriors to enjoy the evening. He thinks always of his people." The warrior grinned at her and exited the hut to find six boys eagerly awaiting his departure.

"The prisoner is fast asleep as Nani gave him a sleep-ing brew. If he wakes up, send your fastest runner to the Chief and surround him with your five remaining spears to keep him in place. Try not to kill him. Tie him up if you have to, but don't put yourselves in danger and don't let him leave this hut. Understood?"

The boys nodded, their eyes wide and attentive. They couldn't believe their Chief entrusted them with guarding the only prisoner. They were proud of the responsibility and hung on to every instruction.

Nani acknowledged the boys, and they stared after her in awe as she went to her whare for a well-earned rest.

When Nani awoke, she was refreshed and invigorated, for she'd slept deeply as soon as she retired. The day was mercifully free of responsibilities. No more practices, drills, contingency planning or going over options. Her mind and heart felt light.

The villagers slept late after a night of carousing, and her one patient would sleep until late morning. Her greatest treasure, her granddaughter, was safe, fast asleep after a heady evening of celebration, and even snored gently.

Nani smiled, helped herself to leftover food for breakfast and almost skipped out of the village. It had been a long time since she experienced freedom. So Nani set off to find a warm place in the morning sun to stretch and warm her old bones. She sang gently while wandering toward her favourite sunny rocks overlooking the ocean. Nani warmed her back against the rock wall and unwrapped a coconut cake.

The warmth suffused her back, and she ate content, licking her fingers and humming.

The day warmed, so she spread her cloak on the ground and made herself comfortable to watch the waves playing on the reef, one of her favourite pastimes as a girl.

It was hard to believe that only last night, today's quiet ocean witnessed and played a leading role in the drama that had unfolded. She sent quiet but fervent thanks to the sea. Their way of life depended on the ocean for sustenance and the supply of materials for medicine, art, inspiration and spiritual cleansing.

"I am becoming old, and I would like to die here and be committed to the waves I have loved and watched so often."

Her grandmother sat in front of her, just as Nani remembered her, smiling her inscrutable smile.

"You will make a long journey, guided by the ocean and the stars. Your work is not yet done, and the years sit lightly on you, my child. When Earth Mother groans and the sea churns, you must take our people to a new place, or our line will diminish, and our ancestors will be forgotten."

And so a prophecy was delivered to Nani on a bright sunny morning. Her grandmother vanished, leaving echoes in Nani's mind.

Nani sat quietly, thinking about her grandmother's words as a cloud scudded across the face of the sun, momentarily blocking its warmth. The responsibilities of a spirit guide were many, and often, such gifts were not given lightly. It seemed that her longing for the afterworld and all those that she had lost would have to wait.

The years sat upon her lightly, and while her grey hair had appeared early, adding weight to her wisdom in the eyes of the younger villagers, her body was still supple and moved well enough. Her mind was still nimble. The climate was mild, and food was plentiful and varied thanks to Marama's gathering and cooking. Life was mostly peaceful. She would need to discuss the prophecy with the Chief, but Nani also decided to allow him a morning of freedom. He certainly deserved it. Not many Leaders would have had the humility to discuss plans with an old woman and a girl or to trust the Gods and spirits as he had.

The weight of responsibility for the village always sat on his broad shoulders. He remained an inspired Leader and had been the Chief for a long time, primarily because nobody emerged as a successor.

Nani had noticed that the Chief spent as much time grooming Tane as his own sons and knew he observed the complex mind behind Tane's mischief. Aue! Why had Tane fallen in battle? Still, it was not her place to question fate or lament what had passed. She must focus on unravelling the prophecy and contemplating what to do.

The thought of leaving home at her age was daunting enough, and Nani received the prophecy. Generally, people didn't want to listen to what they did not want to hear. Let alone set off on a journey to who knows where.

Many days would be spent communicating with the ancestors to understand what would come. The sun was tracked high in the sky, and it was becoming too hot to sit in the sun. Nani took the track back to the village; she should look in on the navigator. Pausing mid-stride, she looked at the sea again.

"Did you save him for this purpose?" she asked the sea.

The waves hissed and lapped, sighing in response to her question.

One of the Chief's older sons and a carver relieved the boys of their guard duties. The young man's eyes were bloodshot, speaking of a late night and good time the night before.

The carver was polishing his spear lovingly, clearly in better shape than his companion. He grinned at Nani as she entered the guest whare, now serving as a prison and infirmary.

The navigator slept soundly, so Nani poked the fire, removed her recovery herbs from her medicine pouch, and mixed a brew for the Chief's son.

"Here, drink this. We were all young once, and there's no need to feel horrible all day."

With a grateful look, he took the brew from Nani and sipped until it was gone. The carver smirked and teased him gently, suggesting he'd seen him vomiting under a palm tree on his way home.

The gentle banter and laughing eventually roused the patient from his slumber. His eyelids fluttered before the navigator's eyes opened. Once again, it was Nani's curious brown-eyed gaze that greeted him. She shooed the Chief's son from her patient's bedside and sent him to get some fresh air.

"Good morning; let me examine you and see if the healing sleep worked." She lifted his eyelids and examined his eyes, noticing the movement of his pupils and opened his mouth, looking at his tongue, before thoroughly inspecting his body and wounds.

He lay passively as Nani went about her work. The navigator recalled her words of the evening before and admitted he trusted her. Clearly, he was a prisoner and in no shape to consider an escape from the middle of the village.

If he'd understood the healer correctly last night, he was the lone survivor of the raiding party. Their canoes were smashed on the rocks. He felt lucky to be alive; it was nothing short of a miracle. And he was equally surprised he'd not been killed.

It was their second raid, and their intentions weren't peaceful. Mako was eager to cement his place as his father's successor. He remembered the whisper of foreboding during the parley and his feeling he might never leave the island last night. Actually, his instincts proved correct.

All his comrades were gone. He was still on the island, captured but being looked after by the village healer. They had been defeated again by a group of women, children, a Goddess, spirits, Gods and a set of superior strategists.

The navigator had no idea how the villagers and the Goddess had achieved their victory. Divine intervention, he suspected.

The healer hinted he'd been saved for some purpose by the Gods of the sea, and he could only agree with her.

Realistically his body should have been sucked out to sea on the outgoing tide and dashed against the rocks. He lost consciousness at some point when he was thrown from the waka and remembered sailing through the air. The boom of the waves on the reef, then nothing until he revived and saw the old woman staring at him.

He survived the ordeal without significant injuries, his body felt fine, and his mind was a little fuzzy but functioning reasonably.

"Well, it seems the Gods have saved your life and protected your body. The night could have unfolded in many ways, but it's unlikely any other outcome would have left you unscathed." She raised her brows, questioning. "Please tell me your story. I want to understand your identity and why you were protected."

Nani had made a fragrant tisane, mixed it in one bowl, then transferred into drinking bowls. She sipped her tea first so the navigator could see it wouldn't put him to sleep.

She needed to win his trust if she wanted honesty. The navigator noted the gesture and raised the bowl to his lips. It tasted of sweet herbs and flowers and refreshed his dry mouth.

"Where to begin?" he asked, rubbing his chin thoughtfully.

"At the beginning, of course. I'm a curious old woman, and I like to know everything concerning the Gods, our ancestors and our world. Maybe the answer to your salvation lies in your past. Perhaps it was written in the stars long ago."

Her regard was intense, and Nani leaned forward to encourage him to speak. She waved the carver to sit in the corner, hoping the navigator would talk freely in privacy.

So it was that the navigator, Starman of the invading forces, told his story to the healer and spirit guide of the village they'd planned to plunder.

Starman was born on a tiny atoll of seafaring people. His father and grandfather were voyagers, as their male bloodline was for many generations.

The stories of their sea voyages were legendary, and they ranged near and far for hundreds of years, navigating by the stars. Many navigators returned, but some settled in new places, sending word of how and where they had travelled if they could. His grandfather had also been a spirit walker who talked with the spirits. Grandfather (Koka) was his teacher as a boy and had taken him on many journeys to look at and learn the stars' position and passage. Many spiritual lessons and offerings were made to the Gods with Koka, including an initiation ritual in an underwater sea cave.

Generations of navigators were initiated and buried in the secret cavern to be close to the Gods who determined their fate. On that day, Starman became a child of the God of the Sea. Koka implored the Gods to take care of him, the youngest navigator of their line. His parents had three girls before him, and he was doted on by the whole family.

They lived happily until a raiding party arrived, blown off course and looking for fresh water. Although they were welcomed warmly, given food and resupplied with water and provisions, the beauty of the women and the richness of the pearls their divers harvested were too much to resist. They slaughtered the men, including Starman's father, plundered the village, taking anything of value and rounded up the women and children.

Starman's Koka was in the sea cave meditating when the invasion unfolded. He had confided in his mokopuna that his ancestors called him to the other side.

Starman was unsure if Koka had crossed over in the cave but often felt his presence after that day, especially when he was at sea. As the man of his household, Starman took his father's spear to defend his mother and sisters with all the ferocity his tiny body could muster. This amused and impressed the invading Chief. He ordered the boy disarmed without harm and put him in his canoe.

On the journey from the atoll, the Chief discovered the boy was a navigator. He took Starman into his household, along with his beautiful mother, who he hoped would give him hearty and intelligent sons.

However, Starman's mother pined over his father's loss. She was resented by the Chief's other women who were no longer called to his bed. Ultimately, his mother walked into the sea and drowned herself, leaving him and his sisters to survive as best they could. Parentless, they were more readily adopted into the village, and his attractive older sisters had no problem finding men to establish a home.

Starman grew up with the Chief's many sons and nephews. It meant he had good food, excellent warrior training, and developed finely honed diplomatic skills. The navigator avoided being pulled into the warring factions for the Chief's favour and gained a seat in his waka.

The training Starman had received, his ancestral knowledge, love of the sea, spirituality and developing abilities to read weather and currents saw his star rise as a respected navigator.

He was a boy when the Chief and his sons began taking him on raids as their navigator, and he always guided them home. Starman had no home to return to, and his only family were now part of the new village. So he lived on an island not of his birth, participating in life and the many raids their war-like nature demanded.

However, Starman kept his own whare and the sea and the spiritual world became his mistress. Although women came and went in his life, he could not commit to any of them. Eventually, they moved on. The memory of how happy his parents had been had stayed with him. He never found the connection he sought in a long-term partnership, even though he wanted a son to share his knowledge.

At times, the ocean pulled, calling him to voyage farther afield as his ancestors did. Starman had not made his defining journey yet. His promise and ambition as a navigator were unfulfilled.

He paused here, slightly embarrassed to share such personal thoughts and dreams with a stranger. Nani nodded sagely as if this was information people shared with her daily, which was accurate. As the Chief's two sons with his former favourite woman matured into manhood, they began to shine in battle prowess and strategic intelligence.

Their mother had been the daughter of a Chief from an island far away, and she was matched with a Chief from another isle before being taken in a raid. Born into and mated with a ruling family, the boys' mother was striking and well-versed in politics and diplomacy.

The raider chief came to value her astute observations and sought her opinion to make his decisions. He also admired how she handled his other women, quietly manipulating them into positions below her and subjugating them to her will.

The brothers' ambition to be the next chief and competition for their father's praise drove them to train with a single-minded passion. Their mother encouraged aggression and urged them to outshine their older half-brothers.

A consequence was the creation of a fierce and bitter rivalry between her sons. They both planned more daring raids, trying to impress their father and the other villages of the island, paying homage to their father and his warrior contingent.

The strength of the village warriors and canoes offered protection to the whole island, and the wealth of their village grew over time, swelled by gifts from others, making strategic matches and the plunder from raids. Eventually, with intelligence, natural leadership, and exceptional skills, Mako won the respect of his father's warriors. It elevated him to the position of preferred successor.

Starman maintained a carefully neutral position on leadership and maintained his childhood diplomacy. The chief did not formalise a choice, and the raids and competition continued. Mako's older brother had his supporters, so the village's wealth ballooned.

The failed first raid provided the older brother, Taiko, a chance to undermine his younger sibling's grip on leadership. He convinced his father that he should take his own canoe with warriors to avenge the fallen, as was his birthright.

Secretly, Taiko wanted to steal the prize his brother swore to claim, to prove he was a worthier warrior and perhaps see his brother fall in battle to the enemy who impressed the men.

Taiko assumed his brother exaggerated grossly to distract attention from his failure and the loss of many warriors. They were surprised to be greeted by the vision on the beach, and the men had misgivings when the girl first appeared. Their skin prickled with the presence of spirits.

Advice was divided, but the parley was accepted by Mako, and they were eager to return home.

But Mako was despatched. The fire raged, and the waves dashed their waka on the rocks. Starman found himself alive but a prisoner. He did not know why his life was spared, but he thanked the God of the Sea, his adopted father, and was eager to make a suitable offering as soon as possible.

Starman regarded Nani's thoughtful face. The old woman was a good listener, and she would understand his spiritual needs.

"Thank you for sharing your story with me. I feel that our fates are intertwined. You were freed from the yoke of the raiders yesterday, and this morning, I received a vision and prophecy. I must make a long journey before I die; it will not be easy. I believe you will be our navigator." She patted his hand reassuringly and bustled about, preparing food herself to restore his strength.

Marama awoke late in the morning. Her body tired from the ordeal, the celebration and the dancing, but the sense of satisfaction for avenging Tane warmed her.

Instinctively, she reached for Tane, but his presence was absent. She rose, stretched her limbs, found some leftovers, and gobbled it down, giggling at her voracious appetite.

She needed to check her traps before she ate the village food stores. It seemed that Piki had a new rival to his title as resident glutton. People stirred lazily this morning, but those awake called greetings. Children placed flowers around her neck or hair and hugged her shyly.

Marama didn't see Nani anywhere, so she told the children where she was going in case the old woman became worried. Nani had shouldered worry for several lifetimes. She hadn't favoured the plan but couldn't devise an alternative.

It was becoming warm, and Marama welcomed the shady trees as she headed for her rodent trap. When she approached, she saw a fat catch. On closer examination, she noticed the rodent wasn't plump but pregnant. She put the rodent in her hunting basket, slung it over her shoulder and went to clear her fish traps.

Marama grinned as she emptied her first two traps, full of tasty reef fish. She would be able to make Nani her favourite fish stew. Marama would let the old woman have all the gelatinous eyes she wanted instead of hag-gling for every eye.

When Marama arrived at the third trap, she was sur-prised to find a giant moray eel inside it. She'd never caught one in her fish traps before, only seen them when diving and spearfishing out on the reef.

It had evil-looking teeth, so she didn't take it out of the trap but did not want to kill it. When she returned home, she'd ask Nani what to do with it. She supposed it could have been propelled in on the same wave she and the navigator had been and felt the eel deserved to live.

When Marama arrived at the whare, Nani was busy making something for somebody. Marama interrupted

Nani's work to give her a heartfelt hug, filled with all the love she felt for her. Nani returned her hug, grateful to have the unusual child in her life.

"Nani, I'm making your favourite fish stew today; the catch was good with everything I need."

Marama beamed with pride at the pleasure on Nani's face. "I woke up this morning and felt I should clear my traps. It was an unusual catch, and I want to ask you what to do. First, I emptied the rodent trap and found this fat one, but it's actually heavily pregnant. Then, in my third fish trap, I found a moray eel! I couldn't bring myself to kill it. It probably got washed in on the wave that saved me, so it didn't seem right. I also didn't want to set it free because of its fierce-looking teeth. What do you think I should do?"

Nani wore a faraway look when asking questions of someone Marama couldn't see or was deep in thought.

"We need to go and see Chief Marama. I had a vision this morning and received a prophecy from my spirit guide. The strands of fate are weaving, and I think your unusual catch is part of it."

With that, she picked up the herbs she was mixing for the Chief, grabbed Marama's hand and bustled out briskly, dragging her granddaughter behind her.

The Chief had just returned from a run and swim, and he was thirstily guzzling a bowl of spring water when he spotted the old woman almost sprinting toward him, Marama trailing in her wake. The sight made him laugh, and he nearly choked on the water as it went down the wrong way. So it was that Nani and Marama arrived to find their Chief bent over and coughing his lungs out, eyes watering, momentarily unable to speak.

They were concerned, but the Chief waved them to go inside his meeting whare, and he followed them, still coughing. The three of them were comfortable in the space where they'd conspired, argued and hatched an unlikely but successful plan.

Marama stirred the fire and held her hands out for the herbs Nani prepared for the Chief. It was a restorative mixture to soothe the body, helping with aches and pains and clearing the mind. So, Marama made enough of the herbal drink for all of them.

They'd been through a lot in the last few weeks, and Nani raced around, climbing hills, working tirelessly, and now a vision. Marama longed for long, hot, lazy days swimming in the lagoon as a child and making mischief with her best friend.

Leadership appeared attractive with many benefits, respect, love, good food, and the best their world offered. But those things came at a high price. The burden of responsibility and the workload were relentless, taxing the energy levels of even the hardiest people. Marama's admiration for their Chief and Nani deepened as they worked together.

Many nights, Marama fell asleep while they continued to discuss details and preparations. It worried her they had so little time to recover from their last ordeal before turning their thoughts to the latest prophecy. Marama regarded the Chief and Nani and marvelled that the three of them had become 'they', a collective of minds. She was astounded to be part of that group.

Marama vowed she would try to shoulder a more significant part of the burden, whatever it was, to lessen the load on the other two. As the youngest, she had energy to expend and was training her body to endure hardship. Now, she must do the same with her mind. To become adept at healing, she applied herself and focused on learning and understanding the principles of each area.

The spiritual link must be strengthened as well. Marama needed to learn to call the spirits and read the signs to be of more use. The aroma of the herbs clarified the matter, and she served a bowl to the Chief and Nani in turn.

"Have you recovered, my Chief?" asked Nani.

"I have to confess, I was so surprised to see you running like a child that I choked on my water," he smiled, showing white teeth.

He is still a handsome man, thought Marama. No wonder the women in his household are devoted to him.

"Tell me what caused you to come here in haste. I don't imagine you run for fun as your granddaughter does. I am curious," he said.

A cloud passed over Nani's face, and she looked at them sadly. These two people were dear to her, but she must share the prophecy with them. Nani knew they would share a new, dangerous and controversial problem.

People didn't like to hear news that might disrupt their lives, let alone throw them into complete chaos. They currently held the trust and love of the entire village as they'd worked together to win a remarkable and improbable victory.

Prophecy and the interpretation of them was a less tangible issue. Preparing for something that might happen at an undetermined point was challenging.

"This morning, as I was sitting in the sun eating my breakfast, my grandmother, my primary spirit guide, delivered a prophecy. She said, 'You will make a long journey, guided by the ocean and the stars. Your work is not yet done, and the years sit upon you lightly, my child. When the Earth Mother groans and the sea churns, you must take our people to a new place, or our line will diminish, and our ancestors will be forgotten.' Then she vanished before I could ask her any questions."

Nani paused to let her listeners absorb the words that had landed in their lives as a pebble thrown into a pond.

"Last night, I had an interesting conversation with the enemy navigator, and he was pondering why he'd been saved. He wanted to give thanks to the Gods of the sea. After receiving the prophecy, I went to see him and asked him to tell me his story. He is not from the island of the enemy. Starman was captured as a child in a raid and comes from a long line of navigators and voyagers. He has an unfulfilled ambition to voyage as his ancestors have for generations. I believe we are destined to navigate together. Then, just before we came here, Marama returned to our whare after feeling compelled to check her traps when she woke up.

Today's catch was unusual, to say the least: a pregnant rodent and a live moray eel that Marama didn't want to kill. I think we have been given the appropriate offerings to return to the sea in thanks for giving us the navigator." Nani paused again, gazing into space as she considered how the offerings should be made.

"The prophecy is for you to consider my Chief. If we wait for it to pass, we may be too late to save our people. But the message will be a blow to many, and we must tread carefully. I do not know when this prophecy will happen, but I will try to find out as much as possible. I felt an urgency to let you know events move quickly. I hesitated to come to you this morning as I wanted to give you peace after our recent trials. I wanted to speak with the navigator and mull over the words in my mind as I have not received a message like this before..." Nani spread her hands in a gesture of uncharacteristic uncertainty.

The three considered each word of the message from many different angles. At first, Marama listened to the discussion, but when invited by the Chief to offer her opinion, she engaged actively. She felt animated and alive. They agreed the offerings to the God of the sea, for giving his child to them was an important step. They discussed suggestions to add to Nani's plan. No decisions were made on the actual prophecy. Unanimously, they opted to sleep on the issue before reconvening.

Later, they shared the fish stew, eaten by the fire in companionable silence; Marama made the herbal brew for Nani. Marama looked into her eyes as she offered the bowl to Nani.

"I have made the dreaming brew for us, Nani, as I've seen you make many times. I want to drink this with you tonight. I need you to teach me about the spirit world and the stars as you have taught me about herbs, delivering babies and healing. You need help in the coming days, and I want to be ready. I want you to push me hard to become adept in this area. I have resisted my studies for far too long." Marama hung her head in shame at what she perceived as her failure as a pupil. Nani took Marama's chin and tilted her head to study the girl's face.

"Marama, you are too hard on yourself. You have barely left your childhood and cannot enter the spirit world unless called. I will share all my knowledge, and you will discover new knowledge as always. Let us begin tonight. When you take the dreaming drink, take something physical you are attached to with you to your sleeping mat to help anchor you to the physical world. I like to hold my mixing stone in my hand. It has been passed from healer to healer for generations. Try not to stray too far and too long from your body lest you become lost in the afterworld. You must let your guides come to you. Don't be afraid, but not all spirits can be trusted, so it is best to establish a relationship with a guide you can trust as you did with Tane. There is no guarantee that

Tane will remain your spirit guide. Or if he does, other guides may emerge over time. I always trust my grandmother because I know her and her presence. She is easy for me to communicate with. My grandmother was born with the gift and could always speak with the spirits; she was, and is, exceptionally strong. When the father of her two children fell in battle young, she lived with one foot in each world. So when she crossed to the other side, it did little to her ability. Sometimes, I have been guided by other more ancient tīpuna. This is why knowing your genealogy and understanding exactly who you speak to or travel with is important. I do not know if your father's people will ever come to you or if your parents are on the other side. Tonight, we move our mats together and join hands while we sleep so we are physically together; we may not see each other in the afterworld, but I want to be with you. Would you like to take my mixing stone? You know it will be yours when I am gone?"

"No, Nani, you take it. Perhaps it connects you to your grandmother, and we need her. I have two items in mind. I want to hold the coral necklace Tane made for me and wear the pearl the Chief and his family gifted. The pearl reminds me of the many people I love and how selfless love can make you."

The pair drank the dreaming potion and moved the sleeping mats together. Each clasped the tokens as anchors, and Marama took Nani's hand, kissing it gently before they lay down to dream and look for answers.

Marama sat up. She felt cold. It was still dark, and the air was heavy and foggy. She could hear whispering around her and wondered why so many people were out and about.

"Hello," Marama called softly, "who is it."

The whispering stopped abruptly. A melodious voice spoke.

"Hello, Marama, we have been waiting for you. I am your Nani's great-great-great-grandmother and have come to be your spirit guide."

The whispering began again, buzzing in the background, louder now.

I must have entered the spirit world, thought Marama, and she tried to hug herself but couldn't feel her body.

Nani's great-great-great grandmother, Marama, began working back through the strands of genealogy. She needed more information to know which branch to follow. Nani waited for guides to identify themselves or tried to find out who they were. Apparently, asking the spirits for their name was not appropriate. How could she determine which line this spirit was from - who was she?

"Greetings, ancestral great mother. Thank you for speaking with me. Can it be true that Nani's maternal line reaches out to me, or am I graced by the presence of my great-grandfather's line?"

It was a subtle invitation for the spirit to reveal her name or ancestry. The whispering quietened, then became silent again. A pregnant pause followed as if the whispering voices and Marama waited for an answer.

"My father was the fish of the great sea, little one," she sang sweetly.

Marama thought quickly. She knew of only one male ancestor called Ika, the fish and as she followed the line down and then up from Nani to check, she recalled the name from long ago.

"Can it really be you, Kiriama? From so long ago, you come to greet such a humble and unworthy girl; I am honoured."

The voices began whispering urgently. Marama was glad she couldn't feel her beating heart. She knew of this ancestor. Kiriama had fallen in love with a brave, handsome warrior who loved only one woman. No matter how hard Kiriama tried to win his affection or entice him to her bed, he resisted her.

A spoiled, attractive and talented woman, she was used to getting whatever she wanted and would not give up. Kiriama made offerings to the Earth Mother and implored her ancestors to free the man from the enchantment of the other woman so she could have him. It became an obsession.

While the warrior was on an expedition, Kiriama made food and offered to share it with the warrior's woman and children. When the warrior came home, he found his woman and two children had fallen ill and died. Kiriama rushed to his side to comfort him, but he pushed her away, and in the madness of grief, he threw himself off a cliff.

Kiriama's mother knew her daughter had taken food to the family of the man she desired so desperately. She noticed she was missing poisonous mushrooms from her healing stores.

In her heart, Kiriama's mother knew what her daughter had done. When the mother found her daughter lamenting the man's loss and wailing it had all been for nothing, she told her husband and chief of her suspicions.

Kiriama was sentenced to banishment but, enraged, screamed she would rather die and threw herself off the same cliff, hoping to be reunited with the warrior in death.

A tragic story and potentially a dangerous spirit. Marama must be cautious. She could not cause offence, but it would also be unwise to trust in such an ancient, malicious spirit who lingered so long in this realm. Marama gave silent thanks to Nani, who taught her the stories she knew of their ancestors.

Another voice emerged from the darkness. Old and papery, the voice sounded but comforting as well.

"Marama, my granddaughter's, granddaughter, greetings. I am Manaia, your grandmother's spirit guide."

Marama was relieved to be found by this spirit who named herself and was definitely Nani's guide.

"Marama is honoured to be met by such an old and exalted spirit, Kiriama, but Marama already has a guide for this journey. He has been travelling on this path of fate with Marama in life and death. As inexperienced as Tane is, I fear that we, who are more experienced, may interfere with matters already in motion. I would love to know Marama better; we are closely tied in blood, but I must make way for Tane. Marama was the love of his short life, and he is not ready to relinquish or share their bond."

In this short exchange, Manaia asserted her blood tie to Marama and Tane's right to be the one to speak without giving any offence.

Kiriama's presence disappeared with an exasperated sigh, and the whispering began again.

"Come Tane, I will leave now, and you may speak," said Manaia and then she was gone.

"Tane, I am here and so happy you can speak with me. I am not ready to lose you from my spiritual life as well. Speak to me," she pleaded.

"I am proud of you, my strange, beautiful girl," said Tane.

His voice was muted, like he spoke from far away or underwater, unlike when he had hovered between his life and the afterworld.

"What can you tell me about our journey, Tane? If Nani goes, I must go to take care of and help her, but I want to know what I should do to prepare. The prophecy did not give us much information, but we don't want our bloodlines to perish and our knowledge or skills to be lost. Our ancestors must be remembered and honoured so we will be welcomed into their world when this life is finished. We need your help, Tane," said Marama.

"Listen carefully, please. You may not like everything I say, but I also have a prophecy to deliver. A voyaging waka must be prepared as soon as possible and supplied for a long journey with many days at sea. Earth Mother will warn you that she struggles. You will feel her shaking, and you must leave. Go from the island. When she gives birth, her child will be bright and terrible. The sea will boil, angering the God of the deep. Our people must be far away before he unleashes his anger. Head south, south, always south. Our ancestors have been to a faraway land in the before. It is cold but has food in abundance, and if you take your seeds, it can be more abundant still. The journey will be difficult, and offerings must be made to soothe the temper of the God of the sea and honour the God of the wind. You are correct, Marama. You must improve your knowledge of the spirit realm. Please call for me or the ancestor you wish to speak with when you arrive. You have attracted a curious crowd as usual," said Tane wryly, "even in the spirit world."

This was more the Tane that Marama grew up with, and he was with her.

"One more thing, Marama, you must preserve the line of the healers and star-gazers. You will have a son in the new land."

"But, but I-" stuttered Marama.

"Don't interrupt and listen carefully; it is important. The boy will have many talents; spiritually, he will be our son, yours and mine, the son we never had. You must survive Marama, no matter how rough the sea or challenging the circumstances are. The boy is not the only child you are destined to have, and the healing skills you and Nani hold, accumulated over generations, must be passed on to our people. Be strong, my love." Then he was gone, his presence melting into the darkness before Marama could ask more questions, protest or contradict his words. Nani warned her that the spirits were often capricious and more set on delivering their messages than telling them what they wanted to know.

That said, Tane had given her much information, and she hoped she would remember it all when she woke up.

Marama was pondering how she would return to her body. She and Nani had not spoken about it when she noticed the whispering was gone. Breath stirred on her upper lip. When she opened her eyes, she saw the familiar inside of their whare, limned in the light from the fire.

The old woman was watching her and smiled when she saw Marama's eyes turn to her. She held a bowl and gestured for Marama to join her at the hearth.

Nani's anticipation of events amazed Marama, and she wondered if Nani actually had to go to sleep to speak with her spirits or if they remained linked much of the time; she would ask another day. She wanted to share the information Tane gave her before she forgot anything.

Marama repeated everything Tane told her, apart from the prophecy that she would have a son and other children. She needed time to come to terms with this more personal information. At the moment, she didn't want to consider and could not comprehend why he thought this would happen. Perhaps it was an event far in the future, although it hadn't sounded that way.

Marama told Nani about Kiriama and, as she did so, had the distinct impression Nani knew of the exchange. Nani nodded sagely but looked smug that Marama had escaped the influence of this particular ancestor. She wondered if Nani had asked Manaia to look after her or if Nani saw her.

She wanted to know and understand many things about the spirit world but was also eager to hear what Nani had learned. There was a cough, and then the Chief appeared in the circle of light at the fire.

"I awakened from a strange dream and saw the light from your fire, so I decided to see who else was awake in the middle of the night," he said.

"The spirits are so busy tonight that all three of us have been dreaming. Even you, without the dreaming potion. There is urgency in the messages we receive as they are coming so frequently. I fear the danger may be closer than we imagined," Nani said, shaking her head.

Nani asked Marama to relate the message she received from Tane to the Chief, and his eyes widened. He knew of stories from the past of islands birthing, fire and rock hurtling into the sky. The earth-shaking and other islands were engulfed by huge waves and had ceased to exist. Nani asked the Chief to tell them of his dream.

He frowned. In his dream, he sat in a circle with the previous chieftains of the village, looking down from above upon their people as they slept. One of them patted his shoulder and told him his leadership was needed more than ever before he cleaved the island in half with a mighty blow.

Then he had awoken with his heart racing and intense sadness. Unable to return to sleep, he had looked for company. The Chief and Marama regarded Nani, who had not yet shared her experience.

"The importance of the navigator was confirmed for me. He will play a pivotal role in our people's survival and in protecting his knowledge and ancestors. He will be the last of his family when the catastrophe comes to pass." Nani looked at them, and she seemed troubled.

"Our plans to save our people and make the voyage will be opposed vehemently. Some people will see our departure plan as an opportunity to seize leadership and fulfil long-held secretive ambitions. Chief, your family will be divided. You will be torn in different directions. Still, we cannot survive without you, and you may need to leave behind many you hold dear. I may or may not survive the journey," she looked at Marama's stricken face fondly, "but I am to be buried in the new land. We shall succeed as long as we follow our ancestors' path, honour the Gods, and we three and the navigator remain in accord. Chief, your dream was right; your leadership has never been needed more, and I pledge to support all your decisions whether I like them or not. My role is to supplement the navigator's knowledge of the stars with my own, guide us spiritually and teach all these skills to Marama for the children she will have in the future, as the unborn generations cannot be deprived of our knowledge." Nani again looked pointedly at Marama, this time with love and a soft smile.

Marama blushed. She hadn't told Nani of the prophecy. However, as usual, she perhaps knew more than Marama did herself. Still, she was reluctant to ask Tane for any more information.

She had not long lost her childhood sweetheart, and her mind was rebelling against any thoughts of a sexual relationship with anyone else. The Chief was aware of Marama's acute embarrassment by the pinkness of her cheeks and downcast eyes. He kindly asked her to refill his bowl. Marama looked up gratefully and busied herself with his request, trying to avoid Nani for the moment. On reflection, Marama realised how comfortable she was with these two people and how much she trusted them. Even though they were about to face a dangerous time ahead, she felt glad they would be together.

They had, by default, become her guardians, guiding her through the most harrowing times in her life with more patience and care than she could have imagined. Whatever came in the future, they could face it together. She topped up Nani's bowl as well. The three of them continued to discuss what to organise and debated how best to raise the prickly subject of the prophecy with everybody else.

Chapter 5

The following day, the Chief announced that they would gather at moonrise on the beach to make offerings to the God of the Sea, who had given them many gifts, including one of his children.

This announcement caused a lot of speculation and discussion on the navigator. The lone survivor.

People sensed an aura about him. The guards caught and repeated snatches of conversation between the navigator and Nani. Nani also made her thoughts known to a few cannily selected gossips, knowing they couldn't keep such exciting information to themselves. Rumours spread like wildfire.

Nani was busy with the preparations for the evening, so she asked Marama to check on the navigator and organise his part in the ceremony with him. The navigator was no longer guarded but was asked to remain in or around the guest whare until he'd been properly introduced to the villagers.

Curiosity to meet the one man who survived the invasion, an adopted child of the sea, gnawed at Marama.

The Gods threw them ashore that night, giving them something in common. He became the different one instead of her.

She called a greeting when she reached the guest whare.

"Can I come in?" Marama asked.

When she entered, Marama could see Starman was surprised but remembered how he'd first encountered her and laughed.

"Goddess, to what do I owe the honour?" he asked, smiling.

She was slim, younger than he thought she was on the beach.

Her eyes, however, were even greener in the daylight, so though he tried not to stare, he was unsuccessful.

"I am sorry for my lack of manners, Goddess. I did not come ashore in the first raid, and the first time I saw you, you appeared out of the ground in a circle of fire. I am a humble man who does not understand these things or how you pulled a waka full of wealth from the sea," he said.

"My name is Marama, and although I like to be called a Goddess, today I'm your humble healer. Sent to check on your health by Nani. May I examine you?" she asked.

He nodded his agreement, but she was already leaning in to start his examination. Marama was as thorough as Nani, maybe even a little more so.

She asked him to cough several times and listened intently to his chest, asking him to breathe deeply. He was slightly disconcerted that she lay her ear on his chest while she did this.

His body was firm and wiry, with muscles trained to paddle and steer for hours upon the sea. Marama's red-gold hair tickled his chest horribly while the green eyes watched him intently, unflinching.

Starman's intense fascination with the girl puzzled him as he wasn't prone to forming attachments to women.

For the first time, he understood.

She is unique and, therefore, a collectable for Mako to possess and show off. Perhaps he'd noticed her intelligence. Mako had been an astute judge of character with the instincts of a shark. He was always prowling for a woman to give him the sons he desired, to follow in his footsteps.

In this case, he'd underestimated the girl to his detriment and paid with his life. It was astounding that so small a person defeated such a fierce warrior. One who had faced down all other warriors in a war-like culture to succeed his father.

After she finished the examination, Marama made little clucking noises to herself, put some water over the hot part of the fire and rummaged in her healer's bag.

"I am going to make you some herbs, and I want you to steep them to make a drink in the morning and evening before you go to bed. You are recovering well, but you have water in your lungs. I can hear it when you breathe. I want you to cough whenever you feel it, and it should resolve itself in the next few days."

The herbs will help safeguard against sickness in your lungs while moisture remains. There's no point in surviving a battle in the ocean and then dying of a few drops of water in your lungs," said Marama.

She stated the facts plainly, strode to the fire, steeped the mixture, bundled his herbs into a leaf pocket and handed them to him.

"Thank you," he murmured. "I find it hard to believe everyone is kind to me when I arrived as your enemy. When I woke up, I thought you had saved me to eat later," he smiled. "Did you lose family in the first raid?"

Marama glanced away quickly so he wouldn't see the unwanted tears and tried to regain her composure.

"Yes, I lost the person I loved most."

When she turned to face him, a tear escaped and rolled down her face. A palpable wave of loss and despair emanated from her and washed over his body.

"Why don't you just kill me?" he whispered.

Starman's face crumpled in pain at her grief.

"I already killed the man who took his life. With the help of the Gods and our ancestors, the women and children of the village avenged our dead without spilling more of our own blood. More killing won't bring anybody back. We have much to be thankful for and see you as a gift from the God of the sea. You were spared because you have a purpose in life. We were propelled toward the beach, against the run of the tide, on the same wave.

Your life and fate are woven into ours, according to the spirits of our loved ones. Nani and I have received words of the future and shared the prophecies with our Chief. I see by the expression on your face that you know this for yourself. Tonight, you will be introduced to the villagers properly as part of a ceremony to honour the God of the sea, give thanks and offerings for our unlikely victory and for sending you to us."

The navigator was bewildered. Marama walked the navigator through the schedule for the ceremony. They discussed the part he would play and how best to make his offering. After settling on the details, Marama told Starman of the visions and dreams. She was impressed with his comprehension of the spiritual messages and his acceptance of the part he would play.

While he'd arrived as an enemy, he was about to become a valuable ally. The Chief thought it best if Marama casually shared information with him to gauge his reaction before the ceremony. They assumed he would voyage into the great unknown with them but needed to be sure.

"See, you understand the meaning and clarity of the messages. Will you voyage with us? Those of us who wish to save ourselves, our culture and protect the memories of our tīpuna will travel into the unknown."

"Yes," he said firmly. "I was born for this destiny. It was written in the stars from birth. My Koka spent the earliest years of my life preparing me for this, and I learned much from the raiders' navigators. The journey has been long and complicated, but I will navigate the voyage with your grandmother," he said earnestly.

They returned to the beach where the enemy landed. The villagers came to watch the moon rise and sing their thanks with all their hearts.

Tonight, the beach and path were lined with torches and lanterns. In stark contrast to the sneaking around in the dark last time they were here.

Marama stroked her rock hiding place fondly. Only she, the Chief and Nani knew all the details of how she'd magically appeared on the beach. The Chief began his liturgy of thanks and spoke to the people of his pride in their courage. The mana the women and children had claimed for the village when they exacted vengeance without further bloodshed or loss of life to their people. He spoke of the bravery of his warriors to stand down, to follow the will of the tīpuna when every part of them desired battle. And of the legend, they wove together that night.

"The God of the sea aided us greatly in our victory by smashing the waka against the rocks and delivering two people to the shore against the outgoing tide. Marama, our healer and recently recognised spirit guide and Starman, the navigator and only survivor from the two canoes who arrived on our shores. Why, we have all asked, was this one man saved? Starman is not of the invaders' bloodline but was taken as a child from another island in a raid. He was given over to the God of the sea to be his child and is descended from a long line of navigators.

Now, he has been gifted to us! An epic sea voyage has appeared in our dreams, and we will need this man's skills. We offer homage to the Gods and our ancestors for the favour. Marama and Starman, please come forward with the gift. You shall return one of his children to the sea as he has returned both of you to us. The God of the sea sent one of his children to test our compassion, and love for him is equal to his love for us."

Starman and Marama stepped forward with the moray eel. He held the head with vicious teeth and she the back of the squirming eel. Marama and Starman spoke to the eel, reassuring him he would soon be back in the arms of the reef, his home and wished him happy hunting.

A hush descended as the moray eel was revealed, and a buzz of good wishes accompanied those chanted by Marama and Starman. The eel was released, and he swam in the shallows, basking in his freedom. Almost as if he was bidding everyone goodbye before disappearing into the sea.

"We welcome you to our community, Starman, child of the sea. Here, you are no prisoner. In our home, we do not raid for plunder or lust for blood and the taking of life. Our warriors are brave and fierce. They defend our village with passion and honour, as do our women and children. Will you take an oath to serve me as your Chief and defend our village?"

"I will," said Starman, "and be honoured to do so. I seek only peace and to serve you by practising my craft for as long as my sea father allows me to draw breath."

There was murmuring amongst the villagers. Some believed their thoughts on why he was saved were correct. But there was also disapproval from the families of those who had lost loved ones in the first raid.

"Peace, my people," said the Chief. "I know we lost people we loved in the first raid. We have avenged them many times over in this very spot, 20 warriors for every one of our people. The bloodshed must end, and we return to our culture of love and compassion rather than becoming our enemy. If anybody wishes to express an opinion or disagree, I invite you to speak without reproach. What kind of Chief would I be if I did not respect the views of my people?" he asked.

Some looked down, chastened by the Chief's words, which upon reflection, were wise. Killing the man stolen as a child and given to them by the Sea God would not bring their loved ones back.

"I have a question for the navigator, Chief." It was the woman of one of the men killed. The Chief gestured for her to speak.

"Starman, I have lost my man and the provider for my two children in the first raid. How do I know I can trust you not to kill more of us and escape in the future?" She asked the question with tears in her eyes.

Starman went down on one knee before them and pledged not to harm any of the villagers and to protect them in the future. He explained he did not wish to return to the raiders and that his parents were killed due to the raid on his island. Starman also offered to provide for the women's children and spend time teaching them skills. The woman nodded her ascent stiffly before stepping back from the speaking circle.

The villagers nodded their approval. Even those still grieving acknowledged an eloquent and humble man who had also suffered loss. The God of the sea was wise. Starman was more akin to being one of them than one of the raiders. Nobody else came forward, so with the fate of the navigator decided, they continued with the ceremony.

By now, the sliver of moon was climbing in the sky, and the bay lit up. Nani stepped forward, began her call to the spirits and the Gods, and invited the God of the sea to send his children to receive an offering.

She held aloft the pregnant rodent, a gift from Earth Mother to protect the devoted children of the land to the God of the Sea.

The Chief stepped forward and joined hands with Nani. He took the offering at the water's edge. Wading into the water and drawing his obsidian knife, he gently opened the creature's stomach, allowing blood to drip.

The dorsal fins of reef sharks soon appeared in the water. The Chief removed the young, one by one, from the pregnant rodent's belly and tossed them into the sea, where the sharks feasted upon them.

With an exultant shout of thanks to Earth Mother, he gave new life to the sea. Hurling the body of the grown rodent into the ocean, the sharks fed in a frenzy. The Chief waded out further, and the sharks circled him several times, but when no more food was given, they returned to the reef.

As the Chief emerged from the shark feeding ceremony, Nani led the people in a chant. The women and children prepared to launch the ceremonial canoe, laden with food, flowers, shells and any offerings the villagers thought would please the God of the Sea.

Most artefacts that sank with the enemy canoes were washed ashore on the incoming tide. After diving into the channel at low tide, only a few items were lost.

Some treasured gifts given to the raiders were offered again to the sea in gratitude. No objects were as cherished by people as their loved ones. They realised this when they had the opportunity to repel the invaders without battle. Items once treasured were piled willingly in the ceremonial canoe.

The Chief announced a council meeting in the morning and urged everyone to walk home with light hearts and pride to spend time with loved ones.

As everyone left, he asked Nani and Marama if they would prepare his favourite drink for him in the evening. He would call after his family had eaten and settled for the night. He smiled at Starman and asked him to join his family for a meal. They departed together on the walk home.

Nani and Marama lingered on the beach together, arms around one another, enjoying the quiet and the moonlight.

"This is the calm before the storm," said Nani. "We need to enjoy this time together ourselves."

"How did you and the Chief summon the sharks?" asked Marama.

"I have been feeding them regularly here and in other places on the island since I was a girl with my grandmother and mother. They can smell blood from far away, and we are unafraid of each other. We are too big for them to eat, and they enjoy a free meal," she smiled.

"I caught us some lobsters today, and I am going to prepare us a feast tonight to celebrate our life here," Marama announced.

They wandered home slowly, looking at plants and Nani pointing out the stars on the way. When they got home, Marama prepared her lobster over the coals with herbs and coconut water, making fresh greens in seawater and some starchy taro with herbs. They ate companionably, licking their fingers until they were full. Marama put lobster aside to offer the Chief when he came, as she knew it was his favourite.

It was late when the Chief arrived, and he looked tired this evening. He had wanted to bring the navigator but didn't want to show him too much favour when they were heading for turbulent times.

Marama prepared drinks and heated the lobster and sweet coconut cakes for a late-night supper.

The Chief nodded his thanks. In truth, he enjoyed coming to the healer's whare; it was more peaceful than his own, and nobody competed for his attention.

At times, he slept in his meeting whare for a bit of peace and quiet. Perhaps he was becoming too old to be Chief, but then the dream was clear, and he still enjoyed leading.

His family was often trickier to manage than the village, with too many personalities close to one another. While taking multiple women to his whare was good for his ego and the village alliances, sometimes he wondered if it was worth the noise, chaos and rivalry it fostered.

"Well, here we are again, we three, making plans to avert disaster. I spoke at length with the navigator after our conversation, Nani. He, like you, has knowledge of the stars and currents that will take us to the great southern islands. The provisioning will be detailed; it is a long journey, but we don't know precisely how long it will take. There are, apparently, other islands on the way. Still, the currents may or may not allow us to re-provision depending on when we leave. There is always a risk that we will encounter hostile people whenever we land. There is always fish to eat, but we want to smoke and preserve as much food as possible in salt. Seed crops we have. We need essential tools, weapons for protection, and I understand it is colder in the south, so we must make garments and shelter when we get there. I have called the council to gauge resistance. Where it will come from, how many of my sons decide to stay and understand how many people follow us," the Chief sighed. I want both of you to be at the meeting tomorrow. I need you to watch what I won't see when listening to people speak. You know me well, and the thought of leaving people behind to die fills me with dread. I must do everything possible to persuade people to voyage with us. I would like you both to repeat your visions and dreams in the council meeting so I may observe who needs to be coaxed into coming. If I didn't have the dream or hadn't experienced the depth of your spiritual connections personally, perhaps I would also be reluctant to leave my home because of a prophecy. I understand the challenge proposing this voyage will create. We are asking people to trust us with their lives and leave their homes in blind faith. At first, I worried we would not have enough space in the great canoes, but now I fear we might voyage alone."

He spread his hands in a gesture of unaccustomed uncertainty and frustration.

"I think you underestimate your leadership, Chief. You have led your people through two raids by superior forces, and both times, we have prevailed with obvious divine intervention and minimal losses. Most people prefer to follow strength and reliability. You are correct, but some people will choose to come simply because you do. The fact we both go with you will encourage villagers in touch with their ancestors to follow the three of us. We will persuade everyone we can to come with us. When we are about to leave, some will realise we are firm in our convictions. Perhaps not everyone is destined for the future we make," she said gently.

"Do you have any thoughts to add to our campaign of persuasion, Marama?" the Chief asked.

Marama felt a thrill of pleasure when the Chief asked her for her opinion, and she frowned as she thought what to say.

"I think many young people will come for the adventure. I would, even if I had not spoken to the ancestors. You may need to consider if and how you will take younger people who want to come when their parents choose to stay and don't want them to leave. Families will be divided, not just your family, Chief. Almost all large families will have those who want to stay and those who want to go." Marama shrugged her shoulders.

The Chief and Nani considered her opinion. Her insights were different to theirs. They hadn't considered the voyage an adventure, but she was right. It would have an element of attraction for those who longed for some excitement in their life. Probably in their younger years, both would have been excited by the prospect of a journey in a great canoe. They ate supper, discussed provisioning, and agreed to reconvene after the meeting. All wanted to be well rested, although they suspected they would not be.

When the sun peeped over the horizon, Nani sat drinking her wake-me-up potion. Marama tossed and turned on her mat, chasing illusive sleep. They had vivid dreams through the night when they napped. Marama dreamt the earth opened up and swallowed the entire island. She stood on the edge of a gaping maw, covering her ears so she wouldn't hear the screams of the people falling.

It was more a nightmare than a dream when she thought about it. She was more determined than ever to leave the island. Eventually, she gave up on sleep, joined Nani outside, and made them food.

They had several hours before the council meeting. They busied themselves with daily chores around the whare.

In some ways, sharing their visions would be a relief. Keeping such critical knowledge to themselves was an enormous burden, especially when they did not know when the prophecy would occur.

They dressed for the meeting with more care than usual as they wanted to be at their best to support the Chief in their capacity as spiritual advisors and healers.

Before leaving for the meeting, they sat cross-legged on their mats with eyes closed and breathed deeply to calm their wairua (spirit) and find tranquillity. Then it was time to go, and they hugged and smiled, knowing they were ready.

They had arrived early at the council meeting place, as had the Chief. Nani and Marama prepared the space spiritually for open discussions and debate.

The Chief's council assembled. Eight men he had known for many years. Trained, fought, ate, fished, raised children, taught others with and celebrated happy occasions, commiserated with in times of sadness. The Chief asked Starman to attend, making their number twelve, including Nani and Marama.

Nani opened proceedings and called their ancestors to join them in the council meeting and to guide their thoughts and hearts on the right path for the good of their people.

"Welcome. I called this meeting quickly as I need your counsel more than ever. I ask Nani and Marama to tell you the prophecies and visions they have each received. Strangely, I have also received a message from the past Chiefs of our village. They came together to my dreams, and I am no spirit guide. The messages concern the future of our people and our very survival. They are conveyed with worrying urgency. I ask you to listen, think and then we will discuss, ask questions and debate as we always do. Nani, please begin," he asked.

The vision and prophecy were revealed.

The dreaming discussions with the ancestors were told almost entirely, but Marama kept the news of her children to herself. The faces of the council members were surprised, shocked, serious, scared and thoughtful.

The events and signs were many, and they were overwhelmed. Still, they listened intently, without interruption, as the Chief requested. When all the information was shared, a loud silence descended.

The Chief regarded each man individually, trying to read their expression and body language. He saw Nani's warning coming to fruition in the disbelieving and hopeful eyes of his oldest son, Tama. Best to address this head-on, he thought.

"I know this prophecy is a shock to some of you. Remember how much our ancestors helped us repel the invaders when we implored them to help us. Not just once but twice. Should we ignore their warnings now when they come to tell us of important events because we don't want to hear them?"

The Chief stared straight at his son, who flushed and looked away.

"I want you to have time to digest this information and interpret the messages. I ask you not to share this information yet, as I want us to reconvene the council this evening. Now, I open the meeting for questions and discussion,"" said the Chief, gesturing to the speaking spot he vacated as he sat.

Nobody spoke at first. Clearly, they were processing the news. Eventually, his second in command asked if there was any indication of when the prophecy would happen. They answered as best they could, repeating the signs, what Tane told Marama about preparing a canoe quickly. Nani stressed how alarmed she was at the frequency of the messages. Still, they couldn't give a precise time.

"So, our tīpuna would have us pack up, leave our homes, and set off for 'somewhere in the south,' in our waka. Guided by the navigator of the enemy, we just destroyed because of a vision and some dreams?" Tama asked. Disbelief on his face and voice dripping sarcasm.

"You must understand that tīpuna do not desire the living to leave the ancestral home unless they are in danger of perishing. We did not choose to receive the messages or signs, and nobody wants to consider losing their home, Tama. If our bloodlines die out, nobody will remember our tīpuna," said the Chief reasonably.

The meeting grew quiet again as each council member pondered the prophecy's words, which Nani had repeated several times now. When no further questions were forthcoming, and everyone expressed a desire to think before the evening, the Chief closed the meeting, thanking everybody for their input and discretion.

As Tama left, he cast a condescending glance at his father. Marama thought he looked petulant and sly. Aue! Nani was right again. Just when the Chief needed the support of his sons, his eldest decided to become a sceptic and a schemer. Marama paid close attention to the council members' expressions and body language, as the Chief requested. She was eager to share her observations as the lines of division appeared.

The Chief arrived at the healers whare to eat with them. He needed some peace to think; he'd become short-tempered with everyone at home. He also wanted to hear their observations.

They knew Tama wanted to remain and lead. However, he'd never voiced any ambition to become the chief and didn't excel in any particular area. Tama was matched with the daughter of a leader from a neighbouring village, and it was likely she, being more ambitious than he, had nurtured these aspirations. The problem with Tama taking this position was that it would attract competition for the vacant leadership and detract from the need to leave the island, which meant more men might choose to stay.

Marama noticed one of the other men, whose daughter was also a woman of Tama, had leaned forward when Tama spoke, nodding in agreement, and was likely to side with him.

She also noticed the pain and indecision of the Chief's second in command. His only woman was also from a different village, and he would be taking her and their children away from her family if they left. Nani made her observations and was sure two of the warriors were already committed to making the journey. She suspected they had received signs but only made the connection during the council meeting.

The remaining four council members were bewildered and thinking carefully about the prophecy. They all understood that this journey was difficult to comprehend and were in the throes of digesting the departure.

They were sure there would be more questions and apparent divisions in the afternoon council meeting. Still, they must win over as many council members as possible to travel with them.

The Chief decided to sound the gong for a village meeting immediately after the council dispersed and to address everyone.

Nani and Marama began preparing for both meetings, attiring themselves in ceremonial dress for the occasion. And commencing spiritual rituals to aid the decision-making of their people.

The council meeting went as predicted, with Tama and his woman's father openly declaring they would not leave their home based on a prophecy.

The two warriors Nani had spoken of declared their intention to follow their Chief and the guidance of the ancestors, who protected them so well. The other four announced they needed more time and wanted to discuss plans with their families. Two of them reiterated to the Chief that they had always followed his leadership and never regretted it. The Chief told them he would call everyone together afterwards to give people time to discuss the prophecy. He would not force anyone to leave, but as their leader, he was loathe to leave people behind to die. Nani told the council that before she received her vision, she had expressed her desire to die on the island, an old but happy woman, but it was not to be.

She had to follow the ancestors' guidance and hoped their people would choose to follow and live rather than perish. The words weighed heavily, and Marama hoped they would tip the balance in favour of leaving for some.

The meeting of the villagers was far more emotional. People were scared of the predicted catastrophe and the unknown future. The safe, secure world they thought would go on forever ended abruptly.

The thought of leaving their homes was distressing, as was the idea of perishing. Once again, the Chief gave people time to discuss the prophecy and the myriad of consequences. Nani and the Chief reiterated the earlier points regarding not ignoring their ancestors because they did not want to hear the message. It was not their place to choose what and what not to share.

During question time, Tama expressed his cynicism and willingness to lead any who chose to stay, which caused much mumbling. Many asked questions regarding preparations and where they would go, and those who firmly announced they would follow their Chief and the path the ancestors chose.

Then, the Chief's youngest son stood and asked Marama what she would do in his place. Marama stood, conscious all eyes were upon her.

"I will follow the destiny our tīpuna have decided for me. I possess generations of healing knowledge. I will learn the spiritual and stargazing crafts to pass on to future generations. I must survive, so I will leave. If I hadn't received spiritual dreams and messages from Tane, I would still follow our Chief, who has always protected our people. I am young and have many years ahead of me. I could have died during the raid, but now I want to live," she said simply.

There was more muttering following her answer and plenty of nodding.

The Chief shot her a grateful look when attention was elsewhere. He didn't want all his sons to stay behind and suspected his youngest son would follow Marama anywhere. Eventually, the Chief suggested they adjourn the meeting to allow family discussion and urged everyone to go home. They would reconvene the following evening, and anyone who wanted to consult with him or the spirit guides was welcome to do so tomorrow. Nani led them in thanks to the spirits.

Chapter 6

In the early hours of the morning before dawn, the villagers were awakened by the violent shaking of the ground. They could not stand to see what was happening, and their whare shook as the earth rumbled. When Marama stirred, Nani was awake and sat cross-legged on her mat. They knew this was part of the prophecy and must hasten their preparations.

Earth Mother trembled, and this was only the beginning. They couldn't afford to wait much longer. They needed to leave the island. Once the tremors stopped, the Chief arrived at their whare with a grim, determined face.

"We cannot tarry. People need to make their own decisions. We will provision the canoe today and leave the day after. Is this soon enough?" he asked, worried.

"I think so," said Nani and Marama together. Neither had received any urgent message to flee immediately, and they knew they must prepare for the voyage or perish anyway.

They went together to each whare to check if anyone was hurt or needed comfort. There were a few minor injuries from falling objects, and one of the older men died of heart failure when the earthquake began.

People were afraid, and many asked when they would leave. They all heard the warning from Tane, and the earth was stirring.

The Chief confirmed they would depart soon and sent the younger boys around the village with the message to return to the meeting place at once. The injured were treated, and people gathered. The Chief addressed them.

"It is obvious to me that we must follow the guidance of our ancestors. We must hurry, and we will leave on the outgoing tide tomorrow. Our search is for a lasting future for our children. I have thought deeply about our preparations for the voyage, and we must take care to take only the things we will require the most. Most importantly, I need to know who will stay and depart. Please move to this side if you are coming and the other side if you have chosen to remain and perish," he said.

People separated, and the division was complete. The Chief closed his eyes to mask the pain as he saw many, maybe a third of the village, chose to remain, including two of his sons, two daughters and their mothers. Many remaining were older people who confided they thought they would just take up valuable space and resources when they did not have long to live. They thought it best to die at home.

Marama was right, though; most young people had decided to leave and looked more excited than scared.

The Chief issued rapid instructions regarding what to take and appointed people to organise food, water, weapons, tools, and equipment for fishing, harvesting water, and packing the canoes.

He'd had time to consider the practical aspects of the journey and what they would need. As everybody was preparing to leave, another earthquake rocked the village, increasing the urgency of those departing. The villagers remaining made light of the earth tremors, reassuring each other the earth had moved before. Some of them, however, had misgivings, and many wondered if they had made the right decision.

The village was in a frenzy of preparation and packing, people trying to decide what to take and leave. There wasn't a lot of space for personal belongings.

During this frantic activity was the heartbreak of separation from friends and family, homes and a way of life. Often, minds changed back and forth in both camps, with tears, arguments, and people trying to persuade each other to stay or go. Still, the preparations moved forward at a frenetic pace.

Tremors rocked the island with increasing frequency, increasing the activity. Nani and Starman huddled together, discussing the stars, their passage, the phase of the moon, the prevailing winds and the currents at this time of year.

Marama watched when she could. She was fascinated by Starman's knowledge of where their island was in relation to where they were going. It was surprising how many places he had been.

Lessons must wait until they were on the journey as she needed to pack the healing supplies and tools. It was challenging when she was unsure what would be available at their new home.

When they arrived, she and Nani would need to learn about new herbs, plants, flowers, fungi and sea creatures.

It was daunting and stimulating, but they needed existing treatments for common ailments in the interim. They travelled in close confinement, meaning any illness could spread.

After packing, Marama checked and gathered all her traps and set about smoking her catch. The Chief asked her to take the fish traps to the provisioning master as he wanted to suspend them from the waka on their journey to supplement their line fishing.

They also wanted to take some game traps and make more on arrival. Once this was all done, Marama hurried home to prepare a meal for Nani. She stopped to comfort children upset by all the arguing and talked to people who wanted reassurance.

Eventually, she returned to their whare and fire. She set about making a substantial evening meal, the last on land for some time, she supposed. The roasting meat and fish on the coals made her stomach rumble. Nani and Starman looked up from their discussion to sniff the air.

"Come," said Marama, "we all need hot food, so I have prepared a small feast."

There wasn't a chance to eat or drink since the morning, and they all ate with gusto, appreciating the subtle flavours of the herbs, salt and spices Marama added.

The fish was baked with coconut and lime, the roasted meat salted and rubbed with peppery plants and fragrant herbs, taro was basted in the roasting fat and juices, all accompanied by crispy seaweed.

The meal became an unplanned celebration of life, and Nani prepared drinks to lighten their spirits. They talked about their childhood, favourite food, happy memories and the things they did that gave them pleasure.

Starman was good company, he enjoyed telling Nani and Marama of his journeys, the stars and navigating, but especially of his parents and grandfather.

He couldn't talk about his slain parents in the raiders' village, not even with his sisters, as they wanted to forget the pain of the loss. It would have been unwise to recall their life and how much they loved their family as any hint of risk that they might seek vengeance would have been dealt with brutally.

After the meal, Nani decided to stroll through the village and see if anyone wanted to speak or needed comfort. She also planned to check on the Chief and his household.

Marama said she would clean up and see to the last of the packing. In many ways, they were lucky. They were not divided in their whare but firmly committed to the future.

Even Starman, the impromptu guest, was confident they were on the right path. But in many whare, farewells or differences of opinion were being debated. They would just leave behind anything that they were not taking.

They led a simple life and did not have many possessions. Hence, preparations for them were relatively straightforward in comparison with most households.

"You must teach me about the stars," said Marama gazing to the heavens.

"Then you must teach me something about healing in return." Starman smiled.

"Agreed. So how about we start now. I would love to understand where my home is in relation to the stars. When we are far away, I can look up and see something familiar in the sky and remember where I came from," she said.

Starman stood and held out his hand.

"Come, we will go up the hill away from the light to see the stars more clearly. On the way, you will tell me what you were looking for when you examined me," he said.

They climbed the hill with Marama, giving a lesson on what you can see in the eye's reaction to the light and its colour, the look of the tongue, the smell of the breath, the beating of the heart, the sounds of breathing and the appearance of wounds.

Starman asked a lot of questions, and so he received his first lessons in the rudimentary art of examination and diagnosis. When they reached the top of the hill, they could see the fires in the village below. They looked so comforting and homely.

"It's strange that tomorrow night, those fires will be diminished and worse to think that once the catastrophe comes, they will all be gone," she breathed.

"Our lives are but a fleeting moment in time, a heartbeat of the Gods, perhaps. Amazingly, they are interested in us when we must come and go like seasonal insects to them. We must be careful on our journey to ensure we continue receiving the favour we have been shown so far.

The Gods are fickle, and I have no doubt when the warriors who arrived with me fail to return, they will look to their ancestors and Gods for revenge and blood," he said.

Marama regarded him in the dark. Only his white teeth showed, but she perceived his presence like she could always feel Nani. Nani believed Starman was endowed with spirituality in the same way as they were. They were both easy in his company, considering he had recently arrived as an enemy.

"Come, Marama, sit beside me, and I will show you how to find the island as it sits under the stars," he said, gesturing to the heavens above.

Marama began her first lesson in triangulating an object's whereabouts to the stars' positions. There were so many stars in the sky. Her first task was to find the constellations and particular stars to use.

Nani had taught her basic star knowledge, and Marama was grateful she had done so. She often asked Starman to repeat information or queried how he found this star or that. He found Marama, an excellent pupil who was thirsty for knowledge.

They agreed that wherever they were tomorrow and every day on the journey after, they would repeat the exercise so Marama would understand the movement and passage of the stars to their travel in the canoe.

"My love, it is time," whispered Tane.

Marama sat up straight, straining to hear Tane's voice inside her.

"Starman is willing to lend me his body to create the son we all desire. I know it is soon, but you leave tomorrow, and I am strongest here, in our home. His grandfather also lends me his strength to be part of our creation."

Marama was shaking her head, then realised the last words were spoken aloud, not softly inside her head.

She looked at Starman's face and put her hand on his cheek. He turned his face to kiss her hand and then gently laid his hand on her face.

They looked at each other, in the dark, each longing for one another and moved together, claiming a tentative kiss.

As soon as their lips touched, Marama felt Tane's arms around her, and she clung to Starman's body with a sob.

All of Marama's pent-up love and yearning were released in a tirade of passion that was met in equal measure by her lovers.

Tane's presence was so overwhelming she knew he was there. Showering her with his love. She could also feel the contours of Starman's unfamiliar body and his spirit entwining theirs. It was a rapturous, otherworldly experience that she did not want to end.

It was also a physical experience that culminated in the seeds of creation mingling in her body.

They lay spent together under the stars. Marama and Tane held their connection to each other physically for as long as they could until he faded back into the spirit world.

Starman cradled her body, entirely in control of himself and trying to comfort her with his warmth. Marama clung to him, only just comprehending what had happened and how she felt.

Eventually, Marama smiled as the tension was released from her body. Tane and she would have a son, and Starman and his grandfather would have another generation of navigators to voyage on the oceans, worshipping the Gods of the sea. This child was born of love and would be cherished by the spirits and the living.

"How do you feel?" she asked Starman.

"I feel a strange sense of contentment and slightly bewildered. My grandfather came to me last night and told me you would be the mother of a new generation of stargazers and navigators. I was not expecting everything to happen so fast. Tane asked me if he could feel you physically again one more time, through my body, and of course, I agreed. I wasn't expecting such an outpouring of passion from us all or the child to be conceived now. I hardly know you. And you don't know me, but in other ways, I feel I've known you all my life," he stuttered.

Marama giggled.

"That is so like Tane to leave a little bit of himself with you to keep an eye on me. I hope you don't mind," she said. Unsure how she would feel in his place. "We haven't just taken advantage of you, have we?"

"I don't mind. Tane has a good presence, and he and my grandfather are fond of scheming. Perhaps your Nani as well. I confided in her that I wanted a son to teach my starcraft, and here we are," he said, raising his eyebrows.

Marama remembered Nani had hurried off straight after eating and left the two of them conveniently alone.

She knew her Nani well, and Nani always knew what would happen before it did. Although Marama was sure, she would plead innocence in this matter.

What surprised Marama the most was she had rebelled at the thought of ever having a physical relationship again, and here she was, totally comfortable lying naked under the stars with a virtual stranger.

Tane had been there, and she had to hold onto the beautiful memory of him. Still, she had no immediate desire to physically extricate herself from the situation.

She thanked Tane for the gift of sharing herself again and applauded his choice of man. She did not love

Starman, and he did not love her, but he would be an excellent father. Intelligent and likeable, Marama thought. Starman was also mulling over the events of the evening. He had navigated raiders to this island twice, the second time for Mako to retrieve his prize. Now Mako was dead, the waka had sunk, and he was lying on top of a hill, having just made love to the 'prize' with the help of her dead lover and his grandfather.

Now, it was his turn to snort in amusement at the ridiculous situation that would produce the child he and everyone else wanted. When he shared his thoughts with Marama, they both laughed at the absurdity of life and the warped humour of the ancestors and Gods.

Eventually, they untangled their limbs and patted Marama's flat belly with shy smiles, excited about the prospect of being parents.

They strolled down the hill hand in hand, feeling guilty that they were so happy when many in the village were experiencing a night of emotional trauma. They decided to return to their own whare separately, rather than arrive together and invite gossip.

When Starman and Marama looked at each other, they knew they were glowing with happiness and would not be able to hide it. They embraced in the dark before they reached the village. Starman held her close and stroked her hair, feeling the need to protect and watch over her and their child.

Finally, they let go of each other, and Starman strolled casually back to his whare. Marama insisted he should go first as it was not unusual for her to wander alone at night. People might ask him where and what he'd been doing. To kill some time, she foraged for coconuts to share with Nani when she came home and talked with the children.

The children, so upset at first, were now bored with the constant bickering and debate at their homes. They were happy to tell her what was going on and invite her to play rather than asking questions she did not want to answer.

Marama prepared fruit and soft coconut for Nani's supper and brewed some herbs that she hoped would help them sleep. It was late when Nani arrived, looking troubled, but she brightened when she saw Marama had made them a late supper.

Nani flicked her eyes over her granddaughter as if giving her a quick examination without touching and contentedly settled herself on the mat. Marama raised one eyebrow at Nani, but as expected, the old woman gave nothing away. Smiling to herself as if sharing a joke with somebody else.

"How do things go in the village and for the Chief Nani?" asked Marama.

"Nothing is simple this evening. As we expected, much angst is caused by those who want to stay. Mothers will not leave their children and grandchildren, men will not leave their women, or they want to leave their women. Children wish to depart, and their parents want to stay. Some remain simply to try and become the next Chief, which will cause more conflict. Tama will remain here, so his mother does not want to leave her grandchildren. So, the Chief must abandon his head-woman and grandchildren. His youngest son will follow his father, as will his youngest daughter, so her mother, frightened by the sea voyage, will come even though she does not want to. Tama's brother is considering staying to lead by Tama's side. But he loves his father, and his woman wants to follow the Chief, as she does not trust Tama. Much of the village is the same Marama, but they must decide quickly. Many fear staying behind without the Chief to protect them and without us to guide them spiritually. Still, they are also scared of the unknown. How is the packing going, and how was your evening?" Nani asked casually.

"The packing is finished. We will use the old bowls tomorrow and then leave them behind. I had my first lesson in star navigation tonight. Starman promised to help me find where the island is every night when we are on our voyage," said Marama

She was not volunteering details of the evening when Nani probably knew everything beforehand. The old woman smiled and began humming as she tidied the few belongings that had not already been packed, raising Marama's suspicions further.

Marama served their supper, and they ate quietly, reflecting that their home would be a memory tomorrow. They would be sleeping in a waka at sea. Marama prepared and packed extra rubbing balm and herbs for Nani to ward off the dampness of the ocean breezes. She had carefully packed an old, worn, woven sleeping pouch to give Nani extra warmth at night. They could fit in together, if needed, to keep each other warm.

After supper, they hugged, and Nani momentarily laid her tired head on Marama's shoulder. It was their last night of sleep on their island, and they were drowsy with the sleeping herbs. So they crawled onto their mats. Blissful sleep was ready to embrace them.

The roar of the groaning earth and the ground rippling in undulating waves beneath woke them. Marama instinctively reached for Nani's hand, waiting to be clasped. The earthquake lasted longer than the previous one, followed by minor tremors.

It was almost dawn, and the village was alive as people ran outside to see what damage had been caused this time. A large crack in the earth now ran through the middle of the village, and in the distance, a cloud rose above the mountain at the far end of the island.

"Aue! Mother Earth is trembling, and our home rent in two. We must go before the foreseen bright and terrible birth, and the sea becomes angry," wailed Nani.

"Stow your last belongings, eat a hearty meal and say farewell to those who dare to defy the Gods and remain. Today, we sail brave people and put as much distance between ourselves and our home as possible," boomed the Chief.

Those travelling scurried into action as the aftershocks continued. Some who were to remain had a sudden change of heart. They bundled their belongings, took them to the canoe masters, and made frantic preparations.

Others determined to stay lounged around watching the frenetic activity, shaking their heads, trying to look bored and not scared whenever tremors hit.

The cloud above the mountain continued to grow throughout the morning and the aftershocks continued, hindering activities as the last frantic loading of food and water took place.

Nani, Marama and Starman ate a quick breakfast together. They were busy with prayers and offerings to the Gods and ancestors in preparation for departure.

The Chief and his navigators, including Starman, climbed up the hill to afford them a better view of the currents and the direction of the breezes, plotting a swift escape.

"The pattern of the waves has shifted, Chief. The sets come in an unusual pattern. We must take care when we launch the canoes," said Starman.

"He is correct," said the village's most experienced navigator. "Something has stirred the God of the sea already, and I do not want to be on land when his anger is unleashed."

Just then, another plume of clouds appeared above the mountain, and the earth shuddered violently, sending a shower of rocks down the hillside.

"It is time to go. We may have to paddle harder to make it beyond the reef than if we wait for the full outgoing tide, but I don't want to wait much longer," said the Chief as he turned on his heel and ran down the hill.

The Chief called for everyone to prepare to launch. He turned to his head woman and embraced her as tears streamed down her face.

"Thank you for being the mother of my children, running my household and supporting me through so many years," he said.

In their early years, they had made many plans together for him to take the reins of leadership. Later, they had many responsibilities, and the Chief had other women in the household for strategic alliance or to have more children. They drifted apart over time. Through all this, they still loved and respected one another and never imagined life without each other.

"Come with me," he pleaded. "It is not too late to change your mind. The children don't need you, and I do not want to leave you to die. You will always be my first love," he said, tears threatening.

"You will always be my first love too, but we are no longer close, and I cannot bring myself to leave our grandchildren. I have failed as a mother. I cannot persuade Tama to come," she sobbed.

The Chief closed his eyes in pain, once she would have followed him anywhere. After so many years together, he had failed her at the worst possible moment. He held her tightly to him, trembling. The Chief kissed her hair and face and realised he still loved her.

"You are the love of my life. I love you still. I am begging you, please change your mind. Grow old with me, Ari," he whispered.

"I didn't know you loved me still," she said.

His face was raw, emotions laid bare. Ari blinked her tears away, looked at her children and grandchildren, and then at the only man she'd ever loved but thought she had lost.

"You are my Chief, and I love you. I will get my things, even though my heart is breaking in two," she cried.

"My heart will be lighter to have you by my side. When we get to the new land, you are the only woman I want. Our two broken hearts can help mend each other's, I hope. I am sorry I failed in raising our oldest son." She lay her fingers across his lips and shook her head in denial of this, then turned to retrieve her belongings before she changed her mind again.

These were the scenes playing out across the village and on the beach. There were changes of heart in both directions as the reality of migration and separation from loved ones took hold.

Many tears were shed that day as lives fractured forever.

The two double-hulled canoes were loaded, launched and paddled out into the ocean. They left the only home most of the voyagers had ever known.

The sails were raised, and many watched the island becoming smaller and the people standing on the beach become figures they could no longer identify. They comforted each other by holding hands or hugging one another.

Marama and Nani sat together, and they smiled at one another. They had done it again, answered the call of their ancestors. Once the island disappeared and all they could see was the billowing plume from the mountain, a ripple of excitement ran through the voyagers.

The canoes were propelled forward on a fast-moving current, assisted by a friendly breeze in the hoisted sails. They were sailing for some time when a little head popped up from behind the food supplies. The supplies were stowed early in the morning, and the child rubbed his sleepy eyes. It was the grandson of the Chief, and he made a beeline for Ari as he was hungry.

"Nana, can I have something to eat?" he asked.

"My little turtle, what are you doing here?" she exclaimed, unable to keep the joy from her voice.

"I didn't want to stay behind, there will be nobody to play with me. I want to come with you and my grandfather so he can teach me to be a fierce warrior, and you can make me my favourite food. I hid for a long time and went to sleep," he said.

The Chief and Ari grinned and opened their arms to their little stowaway, overjoyed that he was with them. Nani laughed out loud and clapped her hands, applauding this small child's wisdom and desire to live. His appearance in the canoe amazed and amused everyone, the buzz of conversation and stir of activity broke the sombre mood of their departure.

As the afternoon turned into evening and the sun dipped into the sea, the voyagers saw fire and steam erupting into the sky from the direction of the islands they had left behind.

They fervently asked their ancestors to care for their loved ones and held each other close. The sea began to roil and heave with huge swells where it had been calm and flat before.

Starman asked the Chief to call his paddle men to action and signalled the other navigator to catch a rolling wave.

"Oh, father, God of the deep who has helped us this far and God of the wind who has propelled us so sweetly, we beseech you to allow us to travel on the back of these beautiful waves. We place our lives in your hands," yelled Starman.

His hair flew in the wind and sea spray. He was exultant and youthful in his enjoyment of the wild waves. The sight of him lifted heavy hearts and gave confidence to those unfamiliar with the sea. The swell was unpredictable, but once the navigator steered them on course, they were catapulted forward and grateful to be alive.

Behind them, a neighbouring island erupted spectacularly, spewing lava, ash and toxic fumes across their home island. One side of the volcanic cone collapsed into the sea, displacing the water and causing a massive tidal wave. It washed over the island and built energy in the deep, swallowing islands and coral cays.

The God of the sea vented his anger at the disturbance of his domain in a terrible and merciless show of might. The Earth Mother shuddered and birthed a new island with lava rivers and superheated steam clouds. Luckily for the voyagers, they were travelling away from the wave in the direction the ancestors had sent them - south.

All that remained on their island home were echoes of the lives lived and the detritus and debris that clung to the foliage.

Chapter 7

Marama was surprised by the canoe's speed; she had never imagined travelling this fast across the water, and it was exhilarating, making her feel alive again. She approached Starman with food. He had been working all day with the paddle men steering the course. For the moment, Starman seemed content, and Nani had been watching to ensure he ate.

Any unattached maidens and mothers travelling on the canoe delivered a plentiful supply of drinks to Starman during the day.

Marama frowned at the flurry of attention Starman was receiving, but fathering her child did not make him exclusively hers. Handsome, unattached men did not arrive in their midst every day. He was polite and respectful but didn't encourage flirtatious behaviour as he was busy with the canoe. Marama was pleased with that.

She tried to tell herself it was none of her business. Still, Starman was the baby's physical father and alive. Marama continued to watch him surreptitiously throughout the day.

"If you are to work all day and night, you need to eat, or we may arrive in a new land with only bones for a navigator. Nani orders you to eat," she joked.

Starman smiled at her, his teeth gleaming, and she marvelled at his transformation at sea.

He seemed far younger and in control, like the Chief when he commanded his warriors or presided over the village. Or perhaps like she or Nani when they were healing. She thought the water was where he shone and belonged, a child of the sea most certainly.

Unconsciously, she placed her hand on her belly where she knew the child was and blushed when she saw he noticed. She was happy to see the joy in his face. Of course, he was pleased he was the living father of the child they made with Tane. He could teach the baby his knowledge of the stars and the seas. Starman took the food gratefully and ate hungrily, gesturing for Marama to sit beside him.

"As soon as I am finished eating, we will commence our next lesson in the stars. Locate the island, and you can watch as I set the course for the first watch," he said, smiling.

Marama was intrigued by his knowledge of navigation and eager for the next lesson but grateful for the darkness as she blushed again, remembering the first lesson the previous evening.

'I must get over this,' she thought.

The canoe was a confined space, and everybody would notice if her face turned pink whenever she was around

Starman. Happily, she did not feel uncomfortable with him. In fact, she felt closer to him than ever. He had allowed her to be with Tane one last time.

She regained her composure and faced people instead of turning her face to the sea and the darkness. After Starman drank, he asked her to find the stars they saw the night before on the hill. Marama thought she saw a cheeky glint of amusement on his face. She ignored it and focused on finding the bright evening star and the 'little eyes' in the sky.

Starman could show her how the stars and moon had changed but explained they must make an allowance for their shifting position because they travelled swiftly upon the waves.

Marama gazed into the dark at where they calculated the island lay, and a pang of loss for her home, the memories of playing on the beach with her parents as a child, flooded in.

She felt Starman's hand on hers in comfort and knew she'd somehow shared her feeling of loss with him. He was either observant, sensitive or possibly both. At the moment she was glad to have a friend again, maybe he was too. He had lost two homes, two lives, and all his family members. At least he would have a son, her, Nani, the Chief, and he was already winning the respect of the navigators and passengers with his skill.

She squeezed his hand back and asked how he would set the course for the next watch. So he pointed out the stars and groups visible behind and before him. The next lesson commenced.

During the daylight, Starman showed Marama how to take easterly and western bearings from the rising and setting sun at the beginning and end of each day. It wasn't long before other youngsters on the waka flocked to the navigator to learn about their journey.

The distraction was a welcome relief to the parents as entertaining exuberant children daily in the canoe was more taxing than on land. They were allocated chores, helping with fishing, cleaning, maintaining equipment and food preparation, and lessons, but this did not stop them from mischief or being annoying.

Starman and the other navigators let some older boys wear themselves out on the paddle that steered the canoe. It was heavy physical work that sapped some of their pent-up adolescent energy.

Marama noticed how patient and comfortable Starman was with the children. She thought fondly that he'd make an excellent father, unconsciously cradling her still flat tummy.

Her other spiritual lessons were progressing well with Nani; during nighttime, they often held hands and communed with the spirits, always looking for guidance on how to please the Gods.

Each time Marama entered the spirit world, she was elated to be reunited with Tane. She met other spirits and bonded with a medicine man she called Old Grandfather. He had been the childhood sweetheart of a great-grandmother. Marama found the workings of the spirit world a complicated web of etiquette and information that often perplexed her. Sometimes, she returned believing she'd been given an insight into the future, only to be told by Nani that the spirit had related a story from the past.

Thankfully, Kiriama did not return, but Tane was correct; the spirits were curious about her. Marama often had an audience until Tane or Old Grandfather asked them politely for quiet or privacy.

With so many people aboard the waka, they were mindful of causing any offence to the Gods. Nani and Marama spent many hours planning ceremonies, thanks and offerings. They also helped with the children, teaching them new songs and chants for the rituals.

Nani regaled them with tales of their ancestors, tested them on their ancestry and taught them strategic games to sharpen their young minds. The days turned into nights, and the night gave way to dawn again, so the days passed on the endless ocean.

The people adapted to life at sea, established new routines, learned new skills, and adjusted their behaviours to living in a confined space.

When the wind dropped, the two canoes sailed or paddled in close proximity to share news, the daily catch and call gossip to each other. Marama jumped aboard the other canoe whenever anyone was ill to check them or administer healing.

After seven days at sea, she helped deliver a beautiful baby girl. The voyagers celebrated the auspicious arrival of new life on their journey by singing in the evening.

The baby and her mother were showered with gifts people made or carried from home. The little girl symbolised the hopes of the voyagers that they would also create a new life for themselves when they arrived in the new land.

The regeneration of their bloodlines was continuing. The baby was named Tuakana Marama by her parents as she would be the big sister of all the other babies born in the new village. Tuakana was delivered by Marama under the moonlight of their namesake.

Marama was moved to have her name included in the baby's naming, and she doted on the little girl, feeling her maternal instincts sharpening in anticipation of her child. The baby's mother was delighted to have an enthusiastic and loving helper with her newborn. Marama often ate with them or arrived with items to entertain the child.

After a visit, Marama returned and spied Nani deep in conversation with Starman. The stars had wheeled into view, but clouds were gathering on the horizon, and winds freshened once the sun dropped into the sea. Marama joined the pair to find out what they were discussing. She often found them sharing information and insights about the stars, the winds, the currents and the spirits or Gods and loved to hear them exchanging knowledge.

At the moment, she did not understand it all. Still, she was beginning to comprehend the influence of every component on the others and the myriad of choices made every few hours on the course of the canoes. Starman was the current custodian of a star map developed and handed from generation to generation of navigators. He and Nani also possessed many oral accounts of previous journeys made. They cross-referenced their many stories along the way.

They added their spiritual connections to all the information, which often manifested in strong instinctive notions to choose one course over another. Today, they both looked slightly troubled. So far, the journey had been comfortable, but they were about to encounter some wild weather.

Starman asked Marama if she would ask the Chief to join them to discuss preparations for the rough ride ahead.

Marama scrambled through the waka to where the Chief and his family relaxed once their grandson had fallen asleep. He was a lively little boy with a never-ending string of questions. Ari hugged Marama affectionately when she arrived; they had become close. Marama had been so relieved when Ari changed her mind and decided to join them that she had burst into tears.

The older woman was surprised by Marama's emotional outburst. Ari was pleased her love for Marama was returned, and she was determined to take her under her wing. She had left behind her precious children, the ones she had given birth to, but the Gods presented her with an accomplished daughter. With no mother, Marama was for her and the Chief to love. Ari felt blessed.

Marama told Chief that Starman and Nani were conferring on the weather and asked if he could join them. They both made their way to the navigation area, curious to hear about what was coming. The wind was lifting their hair now and making the ocean's surface choppy.

"Chief, thank you for joining us. Nani and I are discussing the run of the currents and the storm closing in on us from behind, which will bring rain and wind. We must secure everything as tightly as possible to avoid losing any of our supplies or people. The weather is going to be rough, and some will be scared or sick from the movement. The storm presents us with an opportunity to gather fresh water. Nani and I believe we can set a course to run before the storm with the wind behind us. It will take us slightly off the course we have been on, but it will hasten our journey south. We can reset our course to sail southeast when the winds diminish," explained Starman.

"It seems, Chief, that the wind has heard our singing and received our offerings as has the God of the Sea. The people need to be reassured the storm is nothing to be afraid of but is actually a favour from the Gods to aid our progress. Both Starman and I have oral accounts of uninhabited islands to the southwest, and our ancestors want us to pause there to give thanks to all of the Gods. We must, however, take care and put our faith in the

Gods. If we try and turn from the path granted, they may become angry, and we could be lost. I am not worried about this canoe, Chief. Starman will guide us, but perhaps we can lend another navigator to the other waka. And me for spiritual guidance," she suggested.

Marama frowned. Nani obviously had concerns regarding the ability of the second canoe to stay on course with them. The sea had already transformed from a warm and friendly into a turbulent, white-capped maelstrom covering everything in salty spray. She wasn't excited about transferring Nani to the other waka in this weather or being separated from her while riding out a storm. The safest place for Nani was with Starman. The people relied on the two to take them to their new home.

"It is a good idea, Nani, to supplement the other waka, but I think the weather has turned. It would be easier to climb aboard the other waka, as I always do. I am a good swimmer if anything goes awry. While I don't have your spiritual experience, I can commune with the spirits. The people on the second canoe consider me part of their crew. The voyage relies on you and Starman to guide us to our new home. It seems unwise to separate you at such a pivotal point in time," said Marama, looking directly at the Chief. Knowing she put forward an excellent argument. Nani shook her head at Marama, leaving her in no doubt Nani knew of the child, and Starman looked a little pale and tight-lipped.

The Chief noticed the undercurrent of tension flowing between the others and knew he missed something.

He also needed to decide quickly if they wanted to transfer anyone.

Chief was loath to make any decision without Nani's approval. They steered the village together through many things. But Marama's point of view was inherently sensible and compelling.

As Chief, he must consider what was best for his people and the voyage's success. He couldn't risk losing the old woman who, in her own words, was destined to work with Starman to navigate them to the new land.

"Marama and the best navigator you can choose Starman will transfer to the second waka. I will signal them and give orders to make ready. Starman, please brief the transferring navigator," said the Chief.

Nani closed her eyes tight but recalled her oath to follow the Chief and obey him. She did not try to plead her case further.

Nani foresaw her transfer to the second canoe, not Marama's. So she put her faith in Tane, the ancestors and the Gods to keep them safe. A glance in Starman's direction told her he, too, was worried about Marama and the baby being separated from them. He also remained tight-lipped and accepted the decision. Knowing he must obey as sworn. Put the people and successful voyage above anything else.

Marama's quick thinking and persuasive skills were impressive. He would have to keep that in mind when they were raising their child if he was to have any influence.

Nani and Starman took comfort that Tane watched over Marama and that she was favoured by the Gods. Still, they both called on their ancestors for their protection.

The navigator and Marama were transferred between the canoes in a floating basket attached to ropes. It was already too turbulent to bring the canoes close enough to jump as she usually did.

Marama waved and grinned as she was pulled across the gap. Even though she was frequently swamped by the waves, she made it look like such fun that the children were promised they could have a try after the storm.

The second canoe welcomed the arrival of a fully briefed navigator and a healer and spiritual guide of their own. It raised their spirits and gave them confidence as they stowed their belongings and lashed everything down with increased urgency and a bit of excitement.

The storm was closing fast now, and the navigators and paddlers busied themselves, setting the course and adjusting the paddle to the correct depth, signalling Starman when everything was in place.

Marama and Nani each led the people in a chant to the Gods, the wind snatching the words from their mouths as they sang. It engaged everyone in a shared activity and took their minds off the roiling sea.

The weather became wild and stormy. People huddled together, trying to close their eyes and ride along with the constant movement of the canoe.

Inevitably, some became seasick, but there were vessels at hand to empty the contents of their stomach into.

Most people took herbs to chew from the healers to help quiet their stomachs, which helped reduce the number of people in misery. Marama loved the motion of the sea, even when it was chaos, and saw Starman enjoying the waves in the other waka. She grinned and whooped with delight to the amazement of those huddled in fear in the canoe.

Her joy in the elements was infectious, and some children turned their faces up to be washed in the rain, pelting down, making their parents laugh. It alleviated the tension of waiting for the storm.

Waka rode upon the wild sea, running before the storm at the mercy of the elements. Lightening split the sky, thunder clapped and rolled in the distance, rain squalls carried on the wind, and the people hunkered down, praying for protection.

The canoes tried to stay in sight of each other, but this was impossible. The navigator and Marama were steadfast in their instructions to run with the storm. Not to fight the course in any way or try to stay together. Marama let the people see she spoke with the spirits.

When she giggled and yelled at the sky, "I wish you were here too, Tane!" they were comforted that her spirit guide, who had saved them twice before, was with them.

The storm raged through the night and the day. Everyone was tired, battered, and damp but alive. The sun overhead and its warmth were a welcome relief when the clouds finally parted. Winds calmed, and the storm receded.

They could not see the other canoe. Still, at sunset and moonrise, they would adjust their course to head in the same direction and try to find each other's beacons. Nani and Marama searched for each other with their spirit guides. They would rendezvous at the island with the rocky peak they were sailing towards if they could not find each other.

During the day, the relief at being alive, the joy in being warm and dry gave way to a niggling worry they had lost the other canoe.

The Leader of the second waka reassured them it was impossible to ride a storm and stay together. Still, many passengers weren't used to the sea or had never been in a vast expanse of ocean without landmarks.

They fretted. Marama asked the canoe Leader if they could paddle and sing paddling songs to get warm and lift everyone's spirits. She explained that this is what she thought her Nani would do.

He thought it was a good idea and would also help keep everyone busy. Marama talked to some women and joked that Nani would not let her out of sight for too long. Marama had many lessons to learn before they reached the new land.

Then, she entertained the children with fanciful tales, and most adults listened. The villagers believed in Marama and Nani, so the women's fears were alleviated.

The voyagers engaged in everyday chores that provided routine and comfort.

Aboard the Chief's canoe, they were also drying themselves out and enjoying the sunshine. Having their Chief, Nani and the navigator made them feel more confident and secure they could rendezvous with the other canoe.

Nani and Starman were both anxious to know Marama was safe, and the Chief comforted them.

"Don't worry about Marama. She will be safe and reassure everybody else that they can find us again when we are on the same course. We will light the beacons as soon as it's dark," he said.

Chief hugged the old woman. He knew Marama was all Nani had left of her daughter and man and that Marama held the healing knowledge of generations in young hands.

His youngest son, hopelessly besotted with Marama, had been wringing his hands and praying to their ancestors since the storm passed. Starman also appeared worried, and the Chief wondered if Marama captured his heart while he taught her to read the stars.

Although Marama was unusual, she was loveable. He and Ari looked upon her as family. In his bones, he felt the other canoe had survived the night and was somewhere close, bobbing on the ocean. Chief trusted his instincts where his people were concerned.

As the day came to a close, both canoes checked where the setting sun was in the west. As the evening deepened, the course was re-aligned between the evening star and the visible moon. They headed southwest until the pointer stars were overhead to make a correction.

Each canoe was unsure if they were ahead or behind the other. So they kept a moderate speed, concentrating on steering the waka back on the right course.

The youngsters with the best eye-sight were placed in the front, rear and sides of each canoe to spot the other waka's beacon. The small children watched as well, hoping to be the first.

Chief craftily decided to award a prize to the first person who spotted the other canoe from each vessel. He and the other Leader announced this after sunset.

The prize was to be king or queen of their canoe for a day, be waited on hand and foot, be pampered and be able to make decisions on what to eat and when.

This plan created a welcome distraction, keeping everyone eagerly looking for signs. At the same time, light-hearted teasing occurred amongst the voyagers about what they would have other people do for them when they were king or queen.

As the moon waxed and the night dimmed. The children and some of their mothers fell asleep while the remaining voyagers focused on the liquid darkness. Torch beacons were lit at the front and back of each canoe. It created a campfire effect for those on board who weren't actively watching. They began singing. Softly at first, then louder as their Leader reminded them that sound carried well on the open sea. Singing made everyone feel cheerful and optimistic.

"Look, a falling star," squealed one of the girls on the Chief's waka. There followed a chorus of voices who saw a faint light bobbing on the horizon. It could only be the other canoe, surely.

As the light was behind them, they slowed and held their position. Throwing bright burning material onto the torch to create bursts of light and attracts attention. They saw answering flares in return. A signal they had been seen.

The second canoe raised its sail to make speed, and the paddlers set them on the straightest course toward their fellow voyagers. They all sang loudly, now in jubilation at finding one another again in the middle of the ocean. The Gods favoured them, and they sang the praises of the sea, wind, sky, moon, stars, earth and beloved ancestors.

There was much hugging and jumping up and down. Almost all the children woke up in the hullabaloo, and more than a few tears were shed as the waka sailed side by side again. The sea was calm, and Marama and the navigator clambered across to the Chief's canoe. They were greeted enthusiastically by family first, then everyone else.

With wiry arms, Nani clasped Marama to her tightly and stroked her hair as she had always done when Marama was a child. Chief and Ari claimed her next, hugging Marama while their grandson held onto her legs.

Then Starman stepped forward and embraced Marama. He tenderly kissed the top of her head before giving her upturned face a relieved smile before surrendering her to the women and excited children. They wanted to hug her and hear about her adventure on the other canoe.

Only the youngest son of the Chief looked slightly miserable. He had prayed fervently for her life and was ecstatic Marama hadn't perished but had missed his chance to hug her with his parents. Now, she was surrounded by people. No matter how he tried, he was always awkward around her and tears of frustration built behind his closed eyelids. He had hoped that with Tane gone, he might win her affection over time. But he had been on the canoe with her for many days and had not spoken to her. His father saw his misery and put his arm over his bony shoulders.

"Come, son and greet Marama before she starts telling her story to the children," he said gently.

The boy was three years younger than Marama and still shorter than she was. When she clasped him to her breast to return his welcome hug, he was grateful she couldn't see his pink face or silly grin.

The Chief smiled to himself, remembering his first infatuation with an older girl many years ago. He chuckled out loud when he recalled how he had once spied on her bathing. Hugging his youngest son, he rumpled his hair and let him return to the other boys, who argued about who saw the canoe first.

As so many people had called out at once when they saw the light, the Chief awarded the prize to the girl who saw the falling star. It was the star that led their gaze to the light. On the other canoe, one of the navigators saw the Chief's canoe first as everyone else was looking at the falling star. So, the King and Queen were decided, and it was up to everyone to impress them in two days.

People slept well that night. They were all together again and not being tossed about in a storm. The voyage settled back into the rhythm that had become their life.

Marama and Nani slept holding hands but did not walk with the spirits. Just slept peacefully without dreaming at all that they could remember. In the early morning hours, Marama awoke and saw that Starman was again working with his star chart. She went to where he was working and sat down without interrupting what he was doing, determined to find the island location by herself.

Starman looked up at her and waved before continuing with his calculations. She wondered why he had thrown a trailing line out behind the boat. Then she found the familiar stars and figured out where the island must be. Marama wasn't sure exactly where they were in relation to the island.

"Did you find it?" Starman asked.

"I think so, but I'm more sure of where the island is than where I am. What is the line for at the back of the waka?" she asked.

"Sometimes the canoe gets pushed off course by a wave, but the line reacts more slowly, and we readjust our course to stay on track," he said. Just then, a wave hit the canoe's side with a jolt. Marama saw the line was in its original position and the paddle could be adjusted to set course. It almost felt like an example of a lesson, and she wondered if Starman's grandfather had already started training her and the baby. A large fish jumped out of the water with a splash as if responding to her musings, so she sent a silent thank you to Starman's grandfather for the sign.

"Come sit here beside me so I can show you what I am doing," he said. He was setting a course for the island he and Nani mentioned before they decided to ride the storm. Starman wanted to catch the airflow that would drive them in the right direction as they travelled on the southern current. Marama noticed he used many stars and constellations as his map, to know exactly where he was positioned whenever he could see them and the moon to mark the passage of time just as they did when they were on land. These were things she could learn over time.

What was more challenging for her was his knowledge of wind and water currents and how he applied these to where he was on the ocean. Marama would have to be patient and try to commit the knowledge to memory. The season influenced both the wind and the currents. Time evaporated when she was learning his craft, and soon, the sun would rise, but for now, the night was dark, and the canoe was silent. They sat in companionable silence, leaning against each other. Starman took her hand in his.

"I am relieved to have you back, Marama. While I knew you were safe in my head, the thought of losing you and our child haunted me with every breath I took," he said.

"You must not worry about me and the baby so much; his destiny is in motion, and your grandfather is supplementing our lessons," she said, squeezing his hand.

"I want to protect and take care of both of you. We conceived this child in the most unusual circumstances, barely knowing one another. Still, I think we can make a loving home for our child. We are well matched, Marama. Perhaps not in age but in skills and beliefs."

Starman cupped her face in his calloused hand and stroked her cheek with his thumb. "Think about it, please."

He looked into the green-blue pools that were her eyes tonight.

Marama placed her hand on his face and nodded thoughtfully. If she was honest, she was drawn to him, not just as the father of her baby but as a warm and intelligent man. Her pulse was racing, and her whole body seemed to thrum in reaction to the physical contact and proximity. It was confusing.

She wanted him to hold her again. It made her feel safe when she returned to the waka. And although she was resisting it, she wanted him again physically. Not ideal on a canoe full of people, she thought wryly. She didn't understand what was happening to her. Marama wasn't used to having urges complicate her life, and she baulked at the idea of developing feelings for the physical father of her and Tane's baby.

'Tane, is this you?' she accused in her head, but there was no reply. She followed her instincts, leaning into Starman's body and kissing him.

Starman was surprised by the kiss, and a bolt of desire surged through him. He drew back reluctantly. He wanted to give her time to think and hadn't anticipated that she would take the initiative on the spot to test her feelings.

"You never cease to surprise me, Goddess," he said, his voice husky. "I am afraid we are surrounded by people in a waka in the middle of the ocean."

Marama smothered a giggle by placing her hand over her mouth.

He kissed the top of her head in a fatherly fashion as it was all he dared, hugged her close and whispered that she should go to bed.

As Marama returned to her sleeping place, she felt Nani's eyes on her in the dark. When she lay down, Nani took her hand and squeezed it gently. Nothing got past the old woman.

Marama opened her eyes under the water and saw Tane grinning at her. Then they sat on the sand by the lagoon, the palms above and the sun warming them.

"This is a dream, isn't it?" she asked Tane.

"Of course, it is my love. I am dead."

He gestured with his hands in typical Tane fashion.

"Are you angry with me or interfering with my emotions?" she asked.

"Neither. I can't be with you in your world anymore, and I want you to be happy and safe, my love. I awakened you from childhood in the lagoon. Then we were parted so quickly. I will always love you, just as you love me, but that doesn't mean you can't love someone else. Physically, we are worlds apart now, and your destiny is still unfolding," he said gently.

"I have a message for you, Marama. You must look to the ocean and follow your guide. Then look to the sky to show you the way."

Then Tane was gone, leaving Marama to sit up in the bright daylight.

Marama hurried to Nani's side to tell her about the dream before she forgot any of the messages. They both went to find the Chief.

"I didn't have time to ask any questions," apologised Marama. "Why are their messages always so cryptic, Nani?" she sighed in exasperation.

Nani laughed and told her she was privileged the spirits chose to talk. The messages would become apparent when they manifested in the physical world. They would need to keep their eyes open and tell the navigators whose eyes were always on the sea.

The three went to the navigation and paddle area to brief the men. Starman was finally getting some sleep after a long evening spent with his beloved stars.

Chapter 8

The voyage continued with calmer seas, brisk winds and mostly sunny days. The voyagers were content, even though they'd been travelling for many days. The storm highlighted the perilous journey, so they welcomed every fine day. People settled gratefully back into the daily routine. Even the children complained less as they were learning skills from people too busy for them at home.

They learned about carving, fishing nets, weapons, navigating, history, singing, dancing, genealogy, story-telling, healing, cooking, fish, the clouds, wind, stargazing, canoe making, The Gods, spirits, jokes, knots, rope making, games, customs, speeches, art, craft and anything else that might pique their interest or keep them occupied.

The King and Queen for the day was a successful distraction. People encouraged the royals to get others to do the silliest things and have their feet massaged, hair combed, and food fed to them in small bites.

They asked to be entertained throughout the day and awarded their favourite amusement prizes from others.

It was fun and helped the time fly. There was fierce competition amongst the boys to acquit themselves well in their duties. Every four days, the Chief selected five for personal tuition in leadership, strategy and warrior craft—lessons they desperately wanted.

The parents, siblings and relatives became allies as the boys needed the support of their family for selection. It was a clever idea from the Chief to keep the youngsters in line and teach the future warriors some discipline. Everyone was pleased with the positive change in the boys' behaviour.

During these sessions, Marama positioned herself within earshot to learn from the Chief and one day share his knowledge and wisdom with her son. She sat gazing at the ocean; that was how she spotted a dolphin's fin just before it disappeared. Marama stood to get a better view and saw it moving with incredible speed toward them.

"Look", she cried excitedly, pointing in the direction that the dolphin was approaching from. The dolphin leapt out of the water so everyone in both canoes saw it, then disappeared again.

All the children pointed excitedly at where the dolphin had been. They were startled when it leapt out of the water beside them, chirruping as if laughing at them.

The dolphin played between the two waka before swimming ahead and pushing itself up in the water as if standing on its tail.

"Our guide has arrived," said Nani, clapping her hands in delight.

The canoes adjusted their course, followed the dolphin as it cavorted in the ocean, and seemed to taunt them to try and keep up. Eventually, the dolphin was joined by the rest of its pod, and they joined in the fun. Playing in the wake of the sailing waka and entertaining everyone with their antics.

"I can see land ahead!" yelled Starman.

The lead dolphin leapt, chirruping its musical noises before heading off to chase a school of fish.

The Chief thanked the dolphin guide and the Gods of the sea for sending it to them and led the group in a song to honour the sea. The fish traps were hauled in, and all the fish were thrown back into the ocean in thanks. Each person bowed their head to the sea, revering its mercy and unstinting favour.

They were far from land, but being on solid ground was a luxurious temptation. While Starman and Nani spoke of the uninhabited islands between them and their destination, they were not sure they would find them on this journey.

Some voyagers had told of them in their travel accounts, and others had sailed these waters, never seeing them and doubted whether they existed. The excitement was tangible, and the mood shift created by the appearance of the dolphin lifted another notch.

The people paddled and sang, thanking everyone and everything. Making up new songs to express how wonderful they felt. Marama and Nani joined hands, lifted their faces to the sky, thanked their spirit guides and ancestors and asked them to continue to let them know how they could please the Gods.

Starman thanked his sea father and pricked his finger with a blade to offer blood to the deep. He began a chant, which his grandfather taught him as a child. The other navigators had never seen anyone communing with the sea in this manner, and they observed him with deference. He behaved like a tohunga (priest) rather than a navigator and stargazer. Starman's connection with the sea transcended knowledge and craft; it was spiritual instinctive, and they were glad to be navigating this journey with such a man.

They also felt that the Chief and Nani had chosen well when they welcomed Starman. Although they hoped the people left behind were alive as seafarers, they knew all too well the tales of eruptions and the waves created when Mother Earth moved.

The navigators loved the sea but knew many travellers were unused to the rigours of a sea journey. They would be thrilled to land where they could take fresh water and enjoy different food around a hot fire.

The high peak protruded from the blue depths and beckoned them to come closer. At first, it appeared to be a tiny island, but as they approached, they realised it was a mountain they were steering towards. The navigators guided the canoes to the leeward side of the island. They were greeted by a forest in full bloom with vivid red flowers fringing a sandy bay. It looked so inviting they thought they were dreaming.

"Did I die in the storm? Have I gone to the ancestors?" one of the perpetually seasick women asked.

Even the tide was favourable. The canoe sailed far into the bay. Many wanted to swim ashore and be the first to set foot on land, but the Chief called for patience. There was no guarantee the islands were still uninhabited, he cautioned. A scouting party would land on the island.

People agreed. As eager as they were, it paid to be cautious. There was no point in travelling all this way to be ambushed on a beach while invading someone else's home.

Chief chose Marama for the advance party. She was surprised to be selected, but the Chief wanted her to look for plants they could eat or game to trap and anything of medicinal value.

The scouts would look for signs of habitation and fresh water. Chief wanted to utilise time on the island as productively as possible.

This time, Chief noticed Nani and Starman both frowned, even though Marama looked excited at her inclusion in scouting. He knew how capable Marama was and how she could defend herself. It was unlike Nani to be so overprotective, so he decided to ask her what was causing the worry. Nani was dear to him. She had always supported his decisions, and it pained him to cause any stress.

Starman obviously understood the problem, which he found interesting. The navigator had fitted into their lives as if he was meant to be there. The scouting party made ready, and Chief would keep everyone occupied until they returned. He sent divers to look for crustaceans, shellfish, edible seaweed and a group spearfishing. The women and children organised the water and food storage containers. Baskets for provisions when they went ashore and began meal preparations.

Nani continued the spiritual preparations that accompanied landing in any new territory and ensuring they were welcome. Everybody was busy, and the scouting party soon signalled from the beach it was safe to come ashore.

The children lined up on the canoe's sides. They prepared to dive in the water and race for the beach with much laughing, pushing and squealing - especially when their parents lined up beside them.

The hilarity continued when on the beach. People still rocked as if at sea and could unbalance each other with a slight push. Before darkness closed in, they had a lot to do, so people were sent to gather firewood, fetch water from the stream the scouts found, unpack belongings from the canoes, and set up a makeshift camp.

After the long days at sea, they welcomed the frantic activity of the afternoon and evening, stretching their legs by running to complete their chores or just enjoying the freedom of space around them.

The diving parties found lobster, crabs, many rock fish, and sea snails, while Marama discovered tender hearts in the palm trees, spicy herbs and birds to trap. They were all looking forward to a feast on land. Marama rushed to Nani, alive with stories of what she found, chattering like a child.

Nani smiled at her enthusiasm and tasted the various foods Marama wanted her to try, to flavour the food or use medicinally.

"Sorry, Nani, I got carried away with the new plants. Want to bathe in fresh water? I've found several rock pools in the stream. It might be nice to rid our skin of salt for a change," she added.

The upper pools near the camp were delegated for bathing. The lower side pools were for washing garments or utensils. The top of the flowing stream was for replenishing their water supply. Nani, Marama and Ari set off to bathe, giggling like girls as they anticipated having clean hair and bodies for the first time since they left home. Marama found soap plants, and they lathered up and scrubbed their skin.

The fires were stoked, and cooking smells drifted in the air, making stomachs growl in anticipation of the feast.

Everybody sneaked off to bathe during the afternoon. The youngest children swam and washed many times between carrying out their chores. Nobody begrudged them the freedom. They still helped, running messages and doing little jobs here and there.

Marama sang as they prepared the palm hearts gathered, and before long, they sang song after song. Happy to be alive and together. Starman smiled at Marama as he returned from his bath; his hair was wet, and he looked refreshed. He hugged Nani and whispered thanks for her assistance in getting them this far.

Nani patted his face and thanked him back. Marama noticed they'd become friendly, and she was pleased Starman had the approval of the Chief and Nani. The baby would have a proper family.

'Oh Tane,' she thought, 'if only you were with me, my life would be complete.' But Tane had told her they could not be together here, so she was content to have this child.

Starman was busy today, even though the navigators were told to rest, assisting the woman he had promised to provide for. He made a temporary shelter. The woman was, understandably, still cold with Starman. But her children were young and, not knowing any better, played with him in the guise of helping to erect the shelter. Her family noted Starman made good on his promise, and even she thawed a little. He worked with the children, patiently showing them how to do things and having them bring what he needed.

Marama arrived to help after her cooking duties were finished. The children jumped up and down. They loved her and happily poked out their tongues and posed for her as she checked them over.

Before long, they had a fine shelter, their belongings were stowed neatly, and the children munched happily on dried fruit Marama magically produced from her palm.

The Chief asked Nani if she'd prepare one of her restorative concoctions for him. After a rest day tomorrow, he would drill his warriors and stretch the cramped muscles. He needed this for his old body, he joked. Nani came to Ari and the Chief's sleeping area with a bowl of steaming brew. She patiently chatted with Ari until the Chief had finished instructing his warriors on the exercise plans.

"Ah, Nani, thank goodness you have come, or I fear the program I have come up with will leave me feeling like a broken man," he laughed.

"To me, Chief, you are but a fledgling waiting to test your feathers," Nani replied cheekily. Ari retreated, choking on tears of laughter while the Chief shook with mirth.

"I don't know what you put in these drinks, Nani, but they make me feel young again. Do you hear that, Ari?"

"I will hold you accountable to your promises later," shouted Ari from outside.

Nani laughed. The Chief regarded the old woman with twinkling eyes and affection.

"Nani, I've noticed whenever I choose Marama to fulfil duties that involve some risk, it causes you worry. During our days of planning and working together, I have come to respect her competence and abilities. But it troubles me to lay worries at your feet. Starman is also concerned. So please tell me if there is anything I should know when making my decisions."

Nani checked there was nobody else around and told him of the child Marama was carrying. Nani also explained she was waiting for Marama to share details with her, not wanting to pry, especially on the canoe voyage. Her messages from the spirits conveyed that Starman was and was not the father, which Nani did not understand. She apologised for troubling Chief with her worries; she knew he must make the best decisions for all of them.

Marama was destined to have the baby, so she was unlikely to lose it. The Chief nodded, understanding the old woman's concerns, and assured her he would consider Marama's condition before assigning tasks. Nani placed her hand on his in silent thanks.

The Chief wondered if Starman could shed any light on Marama's pregnancy. He thought the two of them well matched. The navigator was a skilled addition to their people. The village would retain the young healer and spirit guide without the risk of an external match in the new land. He would be pleased if they made a home together, as would Ari and everyone else. Many loved Marama for her selflessness and skills.

"Thank you for sharing this with me, Nani. Please keep me apprised of the circumstances of the child. Do I understand you would approve of a match between Marama and the navigator?"

Nani assured him she would. She'd been concerned Marama would hold on to Tane's memory instead of choosing an everyday life, especially when he remained her spirit guide. Nani had observed how easy they were in each other's company and felt their attraction. Still, Marama was fighting it out of guilt. She most probably felt unfaithful to Tane's memory. They decided to be patient and wait for Starman or Marama to confide in them rather than putting any pressure on the pair.

Chief and Nani were content that Marama and Starman might decide to make a life together, and they both approved. The rest of the conversation turned to the next leg of the journey and choosing an auspicious time to leave.

The feast was a great success.

Food was plentiful and delicious, and friendship had grown between the voyagers. Nobody returned to their family whare on the canoe, separating from everybody else, or had any privacy. They existed as one family, relying on and supporting one another.

Piki travelled on the second canoe and now delighted everyone with his eating, dancing and humour. He was a favourite with old and young alike, but the Chief admired his lightning mind most, so he selected Piki for all his lessons. The chubbiness would disappear, and it didn't inhibit his developing warrior skills. The Chief saw many leadership qualities hidden behind his cheerful, entertaining demeanour.

"Come on, Marama, if you want to be one of my many women, it's not enough to be a Goddess. You need to dance at least as well as your Nani," he teased.

"Right, you little showoff, give me your best moves. I am going to dance you into the ground," Marama scoffed.

The dancing became wild and energetic, with more and more people joining in. The children exhausted themselves and were bundled onto their mats while the drumming and dancing continued. The Chief posted lookouts around the island to ensure they weren't surprised by people from neighbouring islands. But the warriors took the lookout shifts with the youngsters so nobody missed the feast. The men enjoyed the task and practised with their weapons. They loosened their bodies for the upcoming exercises with the Chief.

Their Chief was not young, but keeping up with him was never easy, and he wanted them fit when they reached the new land. They did not know how many people made their home there or if they would be friendly or hostile. The Chief would plan for the worst scenario, so they must be battle-ready.

On the waka, the navigators and paddlers carried the bulk of the necessary work, so the scouting, building and guard duties made the men feel useful again, lifting their spirits.

The feast was fast and furious but did not go on into the night as people longed for sleep on solid ground. They were exhausted, relieved, stuffed with food and ready to surrender to heavy eyelids and tired limbs. As the moon climbed in the sky and the stars twinkled, they admired their beauty rather than relying on them to show the way. Marama sat on the sand gazing at the stars above and tried to work out where the island was now.

"Did you find it?" Starman whispered in her ear.

She shook her head and asked him to help her work out where they were. As she hadn't seen the sunrise or the sunset in the west, with the change of course, she was unsure of the stars. Once Starman pointed out the stars she needed, it was easier to figure out. They sat in silence, enjoying the quiet and heavenly peace together.

"You should continue my lessons tomorrow. I don't have much time and so much to learn," Marama said.

"Which lessons?" he teased.

Marama's face flushed pink in the moonlight, and she smacked him on the arm, which made him grin.

"Stargazing, of course," she whispered wide-eyed and looking innocent. "I am not sure what else you can teach me. What do you have to offer?" she said. She placed her face directly in front of Starman's, snuggled into his body and smiled sweetly.

He looked at her sternly; they both enjoyed the teasing, but he wondered how she felt. She'd loved Tane. Nani told him she'd nearly lost Marama after he was killed. When Starman's mother chose to end this life, he knew how miserable and hurt she was, losing his father. Starman was distraught and angry she left them. He was young and adapted to his new circumstances to survive.

Maybe Marama was doing the same for the sake of the child. He bowed his forehead against hers and put his arms on her shoulders.

"Marama, I want us to take our time as Tane will not be with us next time. I know you loved him, and our child is a miracle, but-"

Marama put her hand over his mouth to stop him.

"I want you to understand that I am choosing you for yourself. I will always love Tane, and he will love me. We no longer exist in the same world and cannot be together in this life. He told me I could love someone else as well. He chose you to be the father of our child, but I choose you because I want you," she said.

Starman took her face gently in both hands, searched her face for a second and saw sincerity. He lowered his mouth to hers and kissed her. Holding her closely, he felt her response as she let go of the restraints she put in place to keep her emotions in check. They melted into the forest away from the camp, holding hands, stopping to embrace each other every few steps. Searching for privacy and avoiding the lookouts. The barriers Marama erected were removed. They suddenly could not wait any longer. Fatigue was banished in the face of more primal instincts.

They sat together again on the fringe of the beach. Marama snuggled into Starman. His arms sheltered her protectively, and they shared a look of contentment and a silly grin. Marama could not believe how happy she was when she thought herself unable to go on living a few moon cycles past.

Marama had experienced a lot of tragedy, but she was also favoured.

"We should get some sleep. You have hardly rested on this voyage, and you are tired. Not wearing you out already, am I old man?" she whispered. He tickled her mercilessly in response, and she covered her mouth with her hand to avoid waking the whole village.

"Do you want to tell your Nani about us? As much as I would like to wake up sleeping next to you, I don't want to scare her, and I should probably speak to the Chief as well. I am new to your people, and you are a valuable, beautiful asset," he said, caressing her cheek.

"Nobody has ever called me beautiful before. Only strange, unusual or different," she said. Luminous eyes shining.

"I find you extremely beautiful. Ever-changing like the sea, and if you don't stop looking at me like that, we won't get any sleep tonight," Starman said, stroking the scar on Marama's now smiling face.

"I am not sure I have ever told my Nani anything that she did not know. I am certain she knows of the baby already. When I volunteered to board the second canoe during the storm, the worry on her face confirmed it. Her spirit guide tells her many futures. She knew about you before I did. It is the way of things."

"Traditionally, in our village, the healers and spirit guides choose their own mates with the assistance of the spirits. The Chief accepts that. In our case, though, I'd like the Chief to know and give his blessing. He and Ari are kind to me. We have been through much together, and we are family. We will sneak to our sleeping mats like any young couple returning from a romantic tryst tonight, but let's speak to the Chief and Nani tomorrow. We will be at sea again before we know it, and I want us to spend time together openly," she said emphatically.

So much for giving her some time and space, thought Starman wryly. For an inexperienced woman, she was rather decisive. But he also wanted everyone to know of their new relationship.

The Chief's son and Piki would be heartbroken for a few days. Still, it could not be helped. It would save Starman from rebuffing unwanted advances from unattached women. Being so new to the village, he had no desire to upset or offend anyone. He was still earning his place amongst them.

They closed their eyes when they reached their respective sleeping mats, and sleep descended immediately. They sighed in complete happiness. Nani noticed Marama's return and smiled before returning to sleep.

Chapter 9

The whole village slept late the next day. Even babies who awakened early merely suckled and went to sleep again. Toddlers got up and snuggled close to their parents. The delicious sensation of being on solid, unmoving ground was seductive enough to entice the earliest risers to turn over for a few more winks.

Only the lookouts stirred as they changed shifts, awakening each other quietly before descending into blissful slumber, lulled by the snoring and breathing around them. The day was dedicated to rest in honour of the Gods and ancestors, and the voyagers welcomed the respite.

When people awakened, they tiptoed to avoid disturbing the rest of anybody else. They made a simple meal, took their laundry to the pools for washing or sneaked off exploring or swimming with excited children who had slept for hours.

Nani had retired early and was the first up in the morning. So she made a fragrant tea for everyone as they woke and heated leftover food on the fire. The Chief and the navigators slumbered soundly, and the other voyagers were careful not to wake them, knowing they'd often worked through the night and day with minimal rest.

When Marama finally woke, she stretched languorously, remembering the evening before and smiled, hugging her knees before bounding up to find Nani.

Nani had a coconut shell bowl ready with the fragrant tea and another filled with tasty morsels for her breakfast. Marama kissed the old woman and blew on the tea before sipping tentatively. It was refreshing.

"You look happy this morning, Marama. Did you have a restful sleep?" asked Nani innocently.

"Yes, thank you, Nani, I certainly did. Sleeping in a rocking waka does not compare with sleeping on firm ground. I love the motion of the sea, but last night I slept so well I could have been a tree or a rock," she said.

"I also slept comfortably in the arms of Mother Earth last night," said Nani. "I was only disturbed once by a little mouse scurrying onto its mat very late." She smiled sweetly.

Marama laughed out loud. Nani's subtle sense of humour was as good as a blunt question. She started from the beginning and told Nani everything. Tane's prophecy that she would have more than one child and repeated the words verbatim twice for Nani to mull over.

She spoke of Tane's request of Starman to join with his body to be with her one last time. The creation of their child, the message that Marama could love someone else without changing her love for him and that they could not be together in this life. How Marama was drawn to the navigator from the first time they met. She even told Nani of the exchange between them on the canoe and how confused she was after kissing him. Last night, she'd finally given in to her desire to be with Starman. Told him she was choosing him for herself, not just to be the physical father of their child.

"Nani, it was wonderful to let myself be with Starman. I am so happy," she said. "Do you think the Chief will allow it? Starman will speak to him about us today, and I - well, I really want his approval of the match. I know you always know events before I do, and I see you have also formed a bond with Starman, but the Chief is our leader," she stammered.

Nani hugged Marama, feeling the excitement, joy and anxiety chasing each other in circles.

"Come child," she said, stroking Marama's hair to calm her as she'd always done when she was over-excited, "you know the wisdom of our Chief. What a good man he is. How much he cares about us and how observant he is. I am certain he already noticed the attraction be-tween you, just as I did because he asked me about you yesterday. Chief wanted to know why I was being so overprotective. He places great value on Starman and the skills he will bring to us. He wants you to be happy. I know he will be pleased," she said confidently.

Marama breathed a sigh of relief and hugged Nani, placing the old woman's hand on her belly with a con-spiratorial smile.

"Can you feel him yet?" she asked. "I know he's tiny still."

"Marama, I have felt his essence the moment he was conceived. I know this will be a powerful child in many ways," she grinned back.

Starman was the last person to awake. Nobody was surprised as he slept the least on their journey, usually during daylight hours when the navigation was more manageable, but never for long.

He concentrated when consulting the stars or making calculations. Otherwise, he was always cheerful, enjoying the voyage more than anybody else. People supposed it was because he was a child of the sea, and voyaging was in his blood. Still, they appreciated his diligence in steering them on a good course and regularly consulting with their spirit guides.

When Starman awoke, he was greeted by a meal fit for the Gods. The children found an enormous cache of eggs and cooked snared birds over the coals with Marama on the beach. Marama added lobster and coconut cakes from the feast and saved a massive bowl of Nani's tea.

The children were thrilled to be making a meal for the Chief and the navigators. They carried a bowl of spring water so the recipients could wash their faces and hands and presented the meal sombrely in a procession to each person as they woke. Starman thanked the children as they set each dish down before grinning and running to the beach. He was grateful for the food as his stomach growled in anticipation after he slept into the afternoon.

The Chief saw he was awake and eating, waved, and joined him.

"I trust you slept well after so many nights of navigating our journey," grinned the Chief.

"Looking at the sun's position, I know I rested well and long. Then I find another feast. I actually thought I was still dreaming of food. Won't you join me?" he asked.

"I have eaten my own meal already. However, I am very partial to lobster and want to try the bird meat again. I am wondering how it will taste salted and smoked. The birds might provide a welcome change to fish on the next stage of our journey. Mmm, mmm, that is good. Marama has her Nani's skills with cooking," he said. Deliberately leaving an opening for the navigator.

Starman smiled at the Chief and asked if they might discuss Marama. The Chief nodded as he put another piece of lobster in his mouth, closing his eyes as he savoured the flavour. Starman confessed everything. Right from the moment he saw Marama on the beach. The deep sense of misgiving he experienced, then waking up to Nani regarding him curiously, and the feeling he'd known them both for a long time. His attraction to Marama, Tane's prophecy, and subsequent request to join him to create the son they all wanted. He'd approached Marama, asking her to consider becoming a proper family. Making a home together to raise the child and that she'd surprised him. Marama was decisive and advised Starman they should be together.

"Chief, I am new to the village. People are just getting to know me, whereas Marama is skilled and loved by everyone. We know we are well-matched and want to be a family. But we also want your counsel and approval. Marama considers you and Ari her family," he said candidly.

The Chief grinned, held out his hand to clasp Starman's wrist, and patted his back.

"I am glad to hear this, Starman. Nani and I were discussing this yesterday. We noticed you becoming closer but did not wish to interfere. Everyone will be pleased except for my youngest son, Piki and a few unattached maidens looking in your direction. Don't underestimate your standing with the people on this voyage; they see you working tirelessly and spending time teaching young people. You are well-liked. The birth of a son for such spiritual and skilled parents bodes well for our future. You shared much good news with me today. Another generation of voyagers, healers, spirit guides, warriors and leaders is emerging. Marama lost the will to live not long ago, and Nani thought we might lose her. Those two carry generations of knowledge that are important to the survival of our people. People love Marama for her selfless courage. We cannot lose her.

A chance for her to love again and live a happy life, after all the sorrows that have befallen her, will be welcomed by all," he said.

"Is there anything that I need to do? I don't have any wealth to offer. Are there any customs I need to observe before Marama becomes my woman?" he asked.

"No, we have an uncomplicated culture. Everyone will know you are together when you sleep in the same shelter. You will be congratulated, receive gifts from people wishing you a happy life and a lot of filthy remarks and teasing," he warned with his eyebrows raised.

They continued with their shared meal. The Chief invited Starman to train with them in the morning and discussed the prevailing winds, tides, and currents concerning their departure. Chief suggested they eat with Nani and Marama in the evening to discuss the spiritual aspects of the next leg of the journey and any guidance they had to offer.

"You need to promise me our younger spirit guide will still have time to sleep and dream," the Chief said. His face was stern before laughing at his own joke. "That is mild compared to what you can expect from the rest of your new village," he warned. Starman rolled his eyes heavenward and shook his head. He was about to receive a feast of quirky humour.

After finishing his late breakfast with the Chief, Starman looked for Marama. Only Nani was at their sleeping place, working on her weaving.

"Greetings, master navigator. How was your conversation with the Chief today?" she asked.

"Good afternoon, Nani. It was favourable, better than I dared hope. And you? Are you also happy to welcome

me into the village and your family as Marama's man?"
he asked, squatting beside her.

Nani opened her arms wide and hugged him fiercely.

"You already know the answer to that question, but
if you need to hear it yes, yes, yes! I am going to be a
great-grandmother, and the boy will be exceptional. He
will have a part, the best part, of all of us and many
of those before us. I sensed his spirit from the moment
he was conceived. Can you imagine that? I didn't understand who he was until Marama told me the whole story
this morning. I am ecstatic he will have a proper home
and family life surrounded by love. You are a spiritual
man like your grandfather. If I was younger, I may have
chosen you for myself," she cackled.

They discussed making a private shelter for Starman
and Marama so they would not disturb Nani's ability
to concentrate on communing with the spirits. Nani
laughed aloud, slapping her thigh. Even she was making
jokes at their expense. Aue!

Nani told Starman that Marama's idea of relaxing was
trapping and exploring. She showed him the direction
Marama went.

"Please try and be back in time to eat with Chief and
save some energy for the drills tomorrow, won't you?"
she chuckled.

Starman set off in the direction Nani indicated, hoping he'd find Marama quickly and share the outcome
of his conversation with the Chief. He was filled with
happiness; there was a bounce in his step and an ache

in his body to hold Marama again. The old woman had planted thoughts in his head.

He climbed for a long time and was hoping he hadn't missed her travelling down a different path. Starman decided to walk to the forest's edge, look down over the area below and check on the currents at sea. As he reached the edge of the trees, he saw boulders to his left and what looked like the mouth of a cave.

Curiosity got the better of Starman, so he clambered over the rocks to look inside, and he was not disappointed. It was beautiful. Seams of quartz sparkled in the sunlight that hit the rock. Stalagmites and stalactites formed over many years joined together in places. There was something magical about the place. As he reached the back of the cave, his grandfather's hand descended on his shoulder, like when he was a child.

"Please bring Marama and the boy here with you to sleep tonight. I want to give the child the gift of navigation as I did with you. Our line will be stronger than ever, and the two of you will know a time of great joy," he sighed contentedly.

Then, the warmth of his presence and the touch of his hand was gone. Starman was shaken by the experience as his grandfather had never spoken to him before or manifested his presence so clearly. The spirituality of the exchange moved him.

From the mouth of the cave, in the sunlight, Starman saw a fish jump out of the ocean. Throwing rainbow colours off its scales, he wondered how huge it was that he could see it from high up.

A sign from his sea father or grandfather perhaps, he was starting to feel like this was one of the best days of his life. He marked the trail to the cave entrance as he returned to the track. Starman heard Marama singing above him as he reached the path and turned to meet her, calling her name and hoping Marama was alone.

Appearing out of the trees, with birds slung over her shoulder and fastened around her waist, Starman thought he would never go hungry.

When she smiled at him, the sun rose from the ocean, bathing him in fiery rays. His desire for her pulsed in his veins. How had it happened fast? He could not imagine and did not want to think about his life without her. Starman rushed to embrace her, dead birds and all, kissing her hair lips and laughing.

Marama heard Starman calling and knew he'd come to find her. His voice sounded excited, so she guessed and hoped the conversations with the Chief and Nani went well.

Then she saw him on the path, and her face split in a stupid grin. Marama was thrilled to see him. When he hugged her and the dead birds, she clung to Starman as he laughed, showering her with kisses.

Starman recounted his conversation with the Chief, trying unsuccessfully to contain his relief at receiving the approval of the man they admired and Nani. They were giddy with happiness. Stopping so frequently to hold each other or share a passionate kiss, they eventually wandered off the path, shed the birds and made love again. It was delicious to be alone. Each time they were together, their bond deepened.

Finally, they lay on the ground, arms and legs entwined, leaves stuck in their hair, feeling sated and lethargic. Starman rolled Marama onto her back, touched her belly and kissed her eyes, nose and mouth gently before telling her about the visit from his grandfather in the cave.

Marama rolled over and propped her head on her hand, regarding him as he repeated the message and smiling broadly when he got to the fish.

"That was definitely your grandfather. He has shown himself to me as a fish, too, one of your sea father's creatures. Do you want to show me the cave now before we go back?" she asked.

Starman hesitated, shook his head and suggested they should get the dead birds back to be plucked for dinner or worry Nani. Reluctantly, they untangled themselves and brushed off the flora that clung to their bodies. Laughing together, they picked leaves from each other's hair, knowing people would notice and guess what they had been doing. They knew they were in for a considerable amount of teasing tonight.

Still, nothing could erode their bubble of joy as they walked home hand in hand, each carrying half the bird haul. They paused just before they reached the camp, squeezed each other's hands and strolled casually into the camp.

They barely emerged before the first joke.

"Marama, what a good catch you have today. One of your birds looks alive and a little familiar."

"What did you use for bait?" called a woman coming home with laundry. She waggled her eyebrows up and down at them.

"Starman, have you managed to navigate yourself into unknown and exotic places again," laughed one of the warriors.

When they reached the food preparation area, the village was abuzz with the gossip that Starman and Marama were in the forest together and returned holding hands.

"My heart is broken, Marama. You were supposed to be improving your dancing and saving yourself for me," lamented Piki dramatically, hands on hips. "I would never have welcomed you, navigator, if I had known you would steal one of my future women," he proclaimed. His comments were delivered with a cheeky smile and rude gestures that earned him a cuff on the ear from his aunt.

Starman and Marama's faces coloured, but they smiled and laughed with everyone, eventually making elaborate bows when they dropped the birds. It caused whistling whooping and started suggestive hip-swivelling dancing.

At last, they returned to Marama and Starman's new sleeping place, apart from Nani's. They were set back towards the forest and hung foliage for privacy. However, they still shared a fireplace with Nani. Marama ran to hug the old woman, letting her feel her happiness through their bond before they enjoyed one of Nani's brews and food.

"I better go back and help prepare those birds for cooking. I found some interesting flavoured plants and seeds on this island and some lovely salt in the rock pools, which I will collect more of before we leave. The jokes are just beginning, so I might as well face the teasing from the women," she said, rolling her eyes.

"I have navigation matters to attend to, but I will meet you here before sundown, and we can eat with the Chief. I am sure there are more days of funny remarks to come," said Starman with a shrug of his shoulders.

Nani laughed under her breath, knowing they were correct as she had spent the afternoon coming up with choice remarks to share when they were in company. She observed that, as a couple, they were glowing. A balm to the ache of Marama's sorrows, she sent silent thanks to Tane. Tane reciprocated those thanks and wrapped Nani in the warmth of his spiritual love.

Starman told Nani of the experience in the cave and his grandfather's message. She nodded sagely, explaining this was a special gift. They discussed the significance of spiritual visits, and Starman shared his plans for the evening and sought input from Nani. He wanted to surprise Marama.

While Marama was teased as the women prepared the birds for cooking, Starman and Nani conspired. The sun flamed its last rays on the horizon in a blaze of orange and pink before the trio set off to share a meal with Chief and Ari. The rest of their family ate with friends and relatives travelling in the other canoe.

Marama had taken care with her appearance, having bathed, washed her hair, dressed it with flowers, scrubbed herself clean, and donned fresh garments. She applied the black lining around her eyes, enhancing the green colour. Nani nodded in approval at her appearance. She wore the pearl from Ari, but its lustre paled compared to Marama's.

Starman looked handsome, and he also bathed and dressed. A tall man, towering over the rest of the villagers with angular features and high cheekbones, he pulled long hair off his face and fastened it there. Oiled skin burnished his muscular physique, and he sported unusual tā moko in two different styles. The flowing designs from his childhood initiation resided on his navigating arm, and the detailed symmetrical style of the raiders on his legs, both telling their own stories.

Together, they made an arresting couple. Well matched in their unique backgrounds, skills and beliefs, destined to be together, Nani thought as she observed them fondly.

The unborn child emanated his joy at the love cocooning him. Tane surrounded them all, and Nani sent the baby a surge of pride in his growth, and he returned his pleasure. She realised they'd grown close, and he was but a tiny glimmer of life. Nani chuckled, shaking her head in wonder.

The meal was lively, with the Chief and Ari welcoming the new couple with delight and humour.

"Well, some bees like to sample the nectar before deciding if a flower is to its liking, don't they," quipped Ari.

"And some birds find a mate and make a nest for their eggs together, and others just make up the rules as they go along," said Nani.

The Chief snorted. "It also appears one invader was actually successful, but he invaded someone rather than somewhere," he said with a cheeky grin.

The sea birds were delicious, salty and plump. The diners licked the fat from their fingers as they ate, between jokes, ceremonial drinks and the occasional story. The evening passed companionably with lots of laughter.

True to her word, Nani produced saucy comments and subtle sexual innuendos to spice up the evening, leaving them all crying. In the end, Marama launched a few barbs back at Nani about being a pupil of the best and following the example of her role model.

Hours slid by. Starman coughed; it was getting late. He announced he had a surprise for Marama, and they must leave the camp. This resulted in more jibes about the size or impatience of his 'surprise'.

Finally, they exited the camp arm in arm, accompanied by whistles and shouts of encouragement from all and sundry. The moon was out early, fittingly for her namesake, as the couple headed off for what was akin to their honeymoon.

Their relationship was more than a dalliance now. They had publicly displayed their intention to make a home and life together in front of the entire village, blessed by close relatives.

Starman led the way, following the trail in the moonlight, holding Marama's hand. They laughed and chatted easily as they walked, filling each other in on the comments received when they were apart. Starman left the trail at his first marker and followed the path to the cave before asking Marama to close her eyes and wait for him.

When Starman returned, he looked pleased with himself, and Marama quirked an eyebrow in question at him. He took her by the hand and led her to the cave.

It was lit by torches and lanterns, illuminating the crystals and creating a magical atmosphere. It was romantic, and Marama gasped, delighted - placing her hand over her mouth. She hugged Starman tightly with tears in her eyes. He was thoughtful and had made a sleeping place in the middle of the room and a fire on the dirt floor.

"I have some gifts for you," he said.

He had a pouch in his hand and removed a beautifully carved jade pendant in the shape of a fish hook.

"This pendant is made of pounamu. That's what people call it in the land where our journey ends. One of my ancestors, a famous navigator, the first of our line to travel to the southern land, returned with this. It has been handed from generation to generation ever since. I received it from my father, he from his, and so on through time. This design has meaning and significance for seafarers, and now it's finally returning home. I want you to wear this tonight as it will belong to our son. It will aid the child's connection to my grandfather and father so he may receive the gift they wish to bestow while in the womb."

Marama nodded in understanding and bowed her head to receive the artefact. It was smooth and cool on her fingertips, so green, like a dark version of her eyes in shadow. As the artefact touched her chest, a throbbing warmth emanated from it. Energy flowed in waves from the pounamu to her belly. She held arms open to embrace Starman so he could be part of the exchange as generations of knowledge were shared with the kernel of a being who would become their child.

Starman did not feel the exchange as keenly as Marama and the child. Heat suffused his body and the familiar presence of his father and grandfather. As the exchange ebbed, Marama sighed contentment from the child and his ancestors rather than herself. She was the conduit for sharing the gift, but Marama also glimpsed the past rushing by in a stream of information.

When it was over, they gazed at each other in wonder. Starman stroked her belly, already feeling the familiarity of the child. They had no words and held each other, standing. Bodies fused together in the cave joined in the spiritual, the three beings cradled by the love of

Starman's ancestors and Tane. Ever so slowly, they became aware of their own breathing, hearts beating and smiling, their physical selves awakening.

"That was a wonderful experience. I have never felt anything like it, and suddenly, I understand more about navigation. Even though I was just a bystander." Starman noticed she wore a rapt expression when she was learning something significant. "I feel I know you better as well. Know who you are and where you have come from. Thank you for opening yourself and your ancestors to me and the baby," she said. Marama stroked his face.

He captured her hand, kissed her palm, and placed it on his heart.

"I also have a gift for you, this time just for you. I don't have much from my mother, but I want you to have this," he said.

He took another pouch and removed an exquisitely carved wooden comb. The wood gleamed in the torchlight, and Marama saw the intricacy of the designs. It was exceptional in its simplicity. "My grandmother on my mother's side received this from her man, my maternal grandfather, a master carver when she became his woman. It is traditional to the women in my family, always worn when they find a man. I didn't understand why my mother gave it to me before she left us, but now I do. Years ago, an angry but devastated boy wove a pocket in his travel clothes. One of my only keepsakes of my mother, so I could always have her with me. I thought I lost it when I awoke in the village. Nani found the pendant and the comb when she treated me on the beach and kept them for me. My mother wanted my woman to have it. She would have loved you, thought you amazing, just as I do," he declared, placing the comb in her hand. Marama removed the flowers and swept her hair back from her face, fastening some of it with the comb and leaving the rest loose in waves around her shoulders. Her eyes were pools of shining green. She was the Goddess on the beach to Starman but also the woman he loved more and more with each passing day.

"You honour me with your gifts, and I never expected to be loved again. Or to feel for you the way I do. I am your woman, and I will care for and honour you for as long as you want me," she said.

Stepping closer, she drew his face to claim his lips. Their lovemaking was less urgent than the day before, slower and more tender, as they had the whole night to look forward to. They took the time to explore each other's bodies, now teasing one another physically until their need for one another became too hard to resist.

At first, they came together slowly, Starman taking his time and Marama riding long rolling waves of plea-sure inside. But her need for more built quickly. Their movements became faster and more urgent until the pleasure crashed over her, and her body was drenched in sensual spasms.

The night was long and memorable as they discovered what pleased each other most. Starman gave Marama lessons in erotic lovemaking, finding her an excellent and intuitive pupil. Their bodies were devoid of tension and drunk with love when they finally drifted into a deep, dreamless sleep.

Frantic activity began in earnest the next day as the voyagers prepared for the final leg of the journey. After the warrior drills, the navigators worked on the canoes, ensuring they were repaired from the storm's battering. Each part of the structure was checked and tested.

The appropriate thanks, prayers and offerings were made to gain favour and guidance for the remainder of the journey. The distance would be shorter on the next leg. However, Starman and Nani warned the sea and weather conditions would be more unpredictable.

Although Starman was the newest to the group, the other navigators sought his input on all matters and deferred to his judgement and leadership. Starman was comfortable in the role as he'd been the navigator for his chief since he was a boy. Still, he was grateful for the attitude and respect offered by his fellow navigators. It meant a lot to him to have status in his new community to share with his family.

Hunting, gathering and trapping occupied many to replenish food supplies with provisions other than fish. Once the supplies were collected, they needed to be cooked, salted or smoked to prolong their use. Water supplies needed to be refreshed and stowed in the canoes. Ropes and woven baskets were repaired or re-placed, bedding in the canoes aired, and fishing lines, nets and traps mended so the pace was frenetic. The voyagers were purposeful, which felt good, so they sang or exchanged friendly banter as they worked.

Marama, Nani and Chief were entirely focused on the necessary spiritual preparations. They bathed and cleansed the Chief, anointed him with oils, and stood on a platform overlooking the sea. Nani had been led there by her guide. Together, they formed a formidable spiritual group. As they prayed and communed, the trio called the ancestors to them, asking questions, seeking answers, and revering their presence.

The Chief found his skills had sharpened over the time he, Nani and Marama worked together. His connection with Nani was always there, but Marama added a new dimension to his ability. He did not speak with the spirits as the two women did. Chief sensed his ancestors around him, felt definite impulses to act on matters and occasionally, they talked to him in dreams.

Tane appeared to Chief in sleep and told him he was repairing his body to look after Nani and Marama and to educate their son and the navigator. When the Chief awakened, his body was tingling. He felt physically youthful, with no stiffness or pain, just strength and flexibility flowing through him.

He felt so good he had awakened Ari with the passion and ardour of a young lover. His warriors were dismayed during the drills at his speed and stamina, with many younger men struggling to keep up. This was a clear sign that they needed to train much harder.

Marama enjoyed the buzz and flow of positive energy created when she, Nani and the Chief were focused on the spiritual world. The air hummed in her ears as the ancestors whispered secrets and offered advice. She always felt Tane's presence around her. Starman's grandfather also hovered protectively around her and the baby, who was already reaching curiously into the spiritual realm, connecting with his father and great-grandfather. A new presence reached out to Marama, and she turned her focus towards the spirit, hoping for a greeting. She was not disappointed.

"Marama, I am Lani, Starman's mother. You wear the comb, allowing me to speak to you and my grandson. I am pleased to meet you. I never wanted to leave my son, but I knew he would be better off without me, and I longed to be with his father. Please look after my son. He gave the pounamu pendant to you for your son, but he needs to wear it. It longs to return to its home, and the spirit of his exploring ancestor travels with it to guide your journey." She faded into the background again.

Nani opened herself up, boosted by the love and company of Marama and their Chief. She felt herself soar into the next world. Her grandmother was with her, and soon, she was surrounded by many of her ancestors. Earnestly, she asked them what they needed to do to please the Gods on their journey. Nani committed to memory the chants that should be sung and the offerings that should be made before and along the way. Her navigating ancestor told her to look for him when they most needed guidance.

"Granddaughter, you must be vigilant. The lost invaders' ancestors have been summoned and are being guided with malicious intent to seek vengeance. Your granddaughter must be ready for them in this world and the next. The fallen warrior quests for her still," he lamented.

As they reconnected with the physical world again, their hands joined, and thanks were spoken.

Marama rose to prepare a restorative drink and fetched water and fruit. They shared what knowledge they gleaned from the spirit world and planned the spiritual necessities. Nani hesitated as their discussion ended, frowning.

"What is it Nani?"

Nani told Marama and the Chief of the warning that she had received that Mako was looking for Marama and that his village had summoned their ancestors to seek revenge.

The words fell heavily in the open air and weighed heavy on their hearts. They had triumphed emphatically in the physical world, and now they would battle Mako's spirit. Marama placed her hand protectively over her belly to shield the child from malice. She was answered with warmth and love suffusing her abdomen. Marama couldn't help herself. She laughed out loud and told Nani and the Chief the baby was comforting her with his love. They, too, patted her belly, talking to the boy and laughing that the tiniest spark of life managed to turn their thoughts from their fears and dark moods.

They knew to be on the lookout for anything unusual in daily life and would be exposed to mischief when on the sea again.

"Marama, would you like me to speak with Starman about the threat? It might be better for him to deal with this news and his emotions in my company rather than you telling him. Nani, what are your thoughts?" he asked.

"It is a good thought, Chief, to avoid throwing him into a state when he already has so much on his mind. Unfortunately, he knows the enemy well. Now, there's also the baby to think of. Perhaps we could tell him together so we draw him into the protective circle we have woven around ourselves. After all, his son is already in it, along with his woman. The sooner, the better, I think. Bad news is carved on your face, Marama. I fear he will know something is amiss when he sees you. Can you join us for a meal when we get to the camp Chief?" she asked.

The Chief agreed and placed his arm around Marama, protectively drawing her to him. Marama hugged him gratefully, finding strength in his fatherly affection. No wonder Tane wanted him to tutor their son. He was the noblest man Marama had ever met.

As they trekked along the trail, Marama gathered greens and spices for the meal and tried not to dwell on troublesome thoughts. She felt invincible and could not remember being this happy for a long time. A caring family surrounded them so she and the baby would enjoy her contentment.

They would be disciplined in eating well, training physically, mentally and spiritually. Marama would ask Tane to keep an eye out for her and the baby in the other world, and she would prevail. Her mouth set in grim determination. The baby answered her with his own rush of emotion, and she giggled. It felt like he was shaking his little fists in defiance, daring anyone to try and harm them. What have we created? She thought, stroking her belly to calm him. Surely, this kind of interaction wasn't typical at this stage of pregnancy. She shrugged her shoulders and accepted that the baby was good company already.

The Chief had made a wise decision. Marama was impressed that he knew Starman well enough to consider the impact the spiritual warning would have.

Starman had arrived after a satisfying day of preparations with his beloved canoes, and he was buoyant. He was pleasantly surprised to see the Chief had come to eat with them, but as he laid eyes on Marama, he saw the tension in her body as she smiled a greeting.

The Chief did not waste time. After greeting the navigator, he launched straight into the warning Nani received. The old woman picked up the tale first-hand and repeated it to give Starman time to absorb and think. Starman placed his arm around Marama and searched her face for signs of worry but found she was more concerned about his reaction than the threat to her and the child. Of course, she had defeated and killed Mako, but Starman grew up with him. Starman should have been more surprised if the man had not turned into a vengeful spirit than to receive the news that he had.

"I know you are worried, but I want you to know I will be ready. We are all prepared to repel whatever mischief Mako or his ancestors throw at us. Isn't that right, Chief?"

"Yes, Nani works on defences. Tane made some physical repairs to my old body to ensure I am up to training your son," he laughed.

The warriors had complained bitterly after their exercise drills that the Chief seemed to be faster and fitter than ever; many struggled through his energetic routines, and now Starman understood why. They shared with Starman the other messages received, with Marama leaving the encounter with his mother until last so he would have something positive to take to sleep on. Marama opened her palm and showed him the pounamu pendant, with a newly made fastening, woven by her and placed it around his neck.

"With greetings and love from your mother, who did not want to leave you but believed it was in your best interests to do so. Your ancestor is still a part of this. As you know, we may require his assistance as a guide. Apparently, the pounamu wishes to return to its birthplace." she said, looking for his reaction.

"I knew my mother would like you, and I am glad she did not wish to leave us. Thank you. In some ways, she is right. If she had remained the favourite woman of the Chief, my life in the village would have been much different. I would have been another competitor in his household for leadership," he said, frowning.

The pain of losing both his parents had affected him profoundly. Marama wondered if his increased sensitivity was a product of that loss; it was one of his most endearing qualities to her.

They ate and talked about the planning and progress and decided the best time to leave would be the day after tomorrow.

The Chief would announce their departure this evening, give everyone time to finish preparations in the morning and have an afternoon of leisure before the last leg of the journey. Southern temperatures would rise, but they would be cold, especially at night.

When they arrived, they would have the warmer months to find a permanent site for their village and prepare for the cooler months. All the stories of the southern land warned of the dramatic changes in season. To the company's delight, Ari joined them with fruit and cakes, her grandson in tow. The youngster asked many questions and entertained them with the new songs and dances he invented while helping to mend the fishing nets. Marama grinned at Starman, imagining when they would sit around the fire with their little man.

Her belly radiated warmth and suffused her with happy thoughts as if the baby agreed. They went to bed

tired from the day's exertions but content that preparations were going well.

Only the seasick voyagers were apprehensive about
the imminent departure. But even they were excited to
reach their destination and never go to sea again.

Marama and Starman retired first. Ari commented
that they were suddenly depleted of energy these days.
The couple beat a hasty retreat as Nani and the Chief
joined in, laughing at their own jokes and attracting a
few whistles from neighbouring fires.

Ari is right; Marama confided in Starman. They both
could not get enough of one another and were forever
sneaking off for a nap, a swim or retiring early. They
snuggled in their cosy shelter and lost themselves in
their passion. Each marvelled at how perfect they were
together. Wrapped in Starman's arms, Marama drifted
into a peaceful sleep. Her limbs were languorous and
relaxed from their lovemaking. Tugging at the edge of
her consciousness was the familiar presence of Tane
enfolding her.

"Thank you for coming, Tane. We need you more than
ever," said Marama. They were sitting back to back on
opposite sides of a coconut tree.

"Your great-grandmother passed the warning to me
and Starman's grandfather. We are watching for the
enemy and his ancestors. His connection to them is
not as strong as yours. I can offer much protection to
you and the baby in this world," he whispered in her
thoughts.

"I know the spirit world is filled with many malevolent spirits, Tane. We need to be as cunning in this world as the physical. His bitterness drives him. I took his life, Tane, to avenge you and save our village, but in doing so, he lost all his men. Can you warn me if he or they are near? I must shield myself and the baby from the spirit world and harm."

The baby reached for his father, and Marama felt the exchange of love between them and Tane weaving his protection around them both.

"We must be rid of this threat, Marama. Our ancestors ponder how we can achieve this, and Nani is searching for answers with them. I have a chance to exact my revenge, but my first priority is always to protect you and the baby, my love. Please sleep well. The next phase of the journey will be taxing."

Tane faded with the dream of the coconut tree. Marama turned over in her sleep, comforted and snored gently as she descended into healing sleep that nurtured her and the baby.

The dawn saw another frantic spurt of activity in the village as people rushed to finish their chores and preparations to enjoy an afternoon of leisure on land. Marama awakened early feeling refreshed and roused Starman from his dreams with a sensual greeting. This put them both in an excellent mood, which made Nani roll her eyes as she handed them breakfast so they could complete their chores.

Starman wanted to adjust the balance of the steering paddles, and Marama wanted to check her traps and gather eggs to go with some lobster.

They were eager to finish their jobs so they could spend time together in the cave or a swimming hole she discovered while foraging. Marama still asked Nani if she needed help with spiritual preparations. Nani was gazing into space and seemed far away, perhaps in the spirit world already. Nani reassured Marama that today, she prepared alone. Marama hesitated. She had promised to share more of the load. Still, Nani was already gesturing with her hands, eyes closed in concentration and heading toward the beach.

Dismissed from spiritual duties, Marama hurried to her traps on the mountainside, hoping she had another good haul of birds and planning how to cook them. The catch was excellent. Marama was hiking down when she spied a sizeable injured bird. A migrating species sitting on the path. It was injured.

I must look a scary sight to this bird with dead ones draped around my waist and over my shoulder, she thought. Laying down her catch, Marama approached the bird, which sat quietly, exhausted and awaiting death. No energy or inclination was reserved for resisting her approach. Marama could see it had a broken leg, a damaged wing and bloody peck marks on its neck and head. It had been in a fight of some sort.

She whispered, asking the bird what had befallen it and if it would consent to her examining its wounds.

Marama reached a hand out slowly, cautiously, so it did not peck her. Petting its feathered back where it had not sustained any injuries, she examined the bird. The damage wasn't severe, but if the bird did not move, it would be killed by something - food was food. She whipped off her wrap, wound it around the bird so it would not struggle, and placed it in a sling around her neck.

The bird still did not move, blinking at her, looking too tired to resist.

"I could be taking you home to cook you for all you know," she said to the bird. Still, it nestled quietly against her. Marama took the rest of her catch, expecting the bird to struggle at the smell of the blood. It blinked at her whenever she spoke to it.

The irony of rescuing an injured bird while carrying a catch of birds to eat was not lost on her, and she pondered whether she should have shown the bird mercy and killed it. The bird turned to her and looked her right in the eye as if it had comprehended her thoughts.

"Ah, you are alive and awake in your fine feathers, lovely bird," Marama smiled.

She didn't know what compelled her to take the bird home and heal it, but it felt right, and she always followed her instincts, so take him she did. The injured bird was an immediate curiosity for the children, and they were more excited about the live bird than the ones they would be eating, which were no fun at all.

To Marama's amazement, the bird sat still and did not peck any rowdy children who wanted to feel its feathers, asking what happened and what she would do with it. Marama had the children find some nice smooth sticks so she could choose one for a splint for the bird's leg. Heat some water so she could cleanse its wounds. The wing she left for now as nothing seemed to be broken. There was a chance it would mend itself. Marama explained the bird would need rest now, just like people did when they were sick. She would place it inside her shelter, make it dark and hope it would sleep. Perhaps the children could pick a name for the bird so they could greet it properly when it recovered a bit.

The kids ran off towards the beach, shouting their ideas at each other and finding fault with this name or that before plunging into the ocean to carry on with the game. Marama carried the bird and draped leaves around it, making a shaded tent.

It seemed to thank her as it moved its head to the side to regard her. Marama told the bird it was welcome and that she would check on him later. Humming, she went to finish her jobs and hoped Starman's work was going as well as hers.

Marama was finished first and went to see how Starman was faring with his paddle adjustments. She was, of course, greeted with friendly teasing from the navigators, especially when she asked Starman how his paddle was. The navigators dissolved in fits of laughter, tears streaming down their cheeks and clutching their bellies while Marama grinned with pink-tinged cheeks at her own gaff.

"That's it, we are now officially done for the day. My woman has come seeking tidings of my paddle. I have urgent things to attend to," said Starman.

He kept a straight face before grabbing Marama's hand and running off down the beach laughing. Loud whistles and jibes erupted behind them. Starman pulled Marama behind the first outcrop of rocks they came to, crushing her lips and pulling her body against him.

Marama responded and dragged him further off the beach. It was a long morning of separation, and she did not want to be disturbed. She needed him now. They made the most of their time alone on the island. Soon, they would be back on the canoe, focused on tasks and moments stolen together in the dark would be precious.

The couple walked to the waterfall swimming hole Marama had found and indulged themselves in as much carnal pleasure as they could. Still discovering each other and surprising themselves with their insatiable appetite. It was a magical afternoon; with the cares of the voyage parked in another realm of existence, they cavorted like children, teasing each other and laughing.

It was becoming dark when they strolled into the camp happy, scrubbed and clean. Nani looked up at them and smiled indulgently. While she enjoyed teasing them, she loved them fiercely and was protective of their little family.

She made elaborate preparations and offerings to the Gods with the ancestors' help. Utilising her strength to muster forces against the invaders' revenge, she was satisfied she'd accomplished much in one day. Marama had the birds and vegetables cooking in a ground pit all day, and Nani had just removed the food when they appeared. The aroma wafted tantalisingly in their direction, and their stomachs rumbled in stereo as they jogged to the fire laughing. Marama cooked a lot of food and took it to place in the communal eating area for everyone, where she was thanked by people attracted by the smell.

She then took a dish of egg and lobster with spices and the umu-baked birds with vegetables to the Chief and Ari before eating. Lost in their romantic afternoon together, Marama had forgotten to tell Starman about the bird she found. She was surprised when she saw the bird cradled in Starman's arms being fed fish, to Nani's amusement.

"Where did you find him, Marama? This bird is a navigator, just like me. He will be heading south for the warm season soon in the same direction as we travel. He is awfully friendly. I have never one up close, and he was not afraid when I peered into his tent," said Starman. Feeding the bird another fish from the bait basket.

Marama recounted how she found the bird and attended to him, with the children's help, as she devoured her food. She was famished. The bird still blinked as she talked while taking food from Starman's fingers. She and Nani exchanged glances, knowing this was unusual behaviour for a bird, definitely a sign, a positive sign.

The bird sat between Marama and Starman while they ate and groomed himself after his fish meal. The wounds had started to scab nicely, the splint was still on, and the wing could now fold into a more normal position. The exhaustion had also passed. He was a handsome bird. Starman explained to Marama the markings that showed he was male and that his kind fought over mating rights and territory. The bird probably lost a fight but was lucky to escape death.

Marama regarded her new friend because that was how she thought of him. She was pleased she had saved him, especially now that Starman had explained how much they had in common.

"Well, exalted friend, I am inviting you to stay the night in our camp where you will be safe and to join us on our journey when the tide turns tomorrow. What do you say?" she asked.

To her surprise, the bird looked her in the eye and nodded his head in ascent. Nani clapped her hands together with pleasure. She was sure this bird was sent to them for a purpose. So she introduced herself to him politely and offered him a drink, which he accepted.

After the meal, the children started checking on the bird. They were excited he was making such a good recovery. Marama told them they could bring him any spare small fish. They had to ask their parents or catch them for breakfast in the morning, which kept them all happy.

The voyagers retired early for their last night on the island. They all wanted to enjoy sleeping on solid ground before they returned to the rocking motion of the canoe and life at sea. Even the children were happy to go to sleep for once. Still, they had enjoyed a free afternoon of energetic play, swimming and games without any chores or adults telling them what to do, nirvana.

Chapter 10

Dawn found the voyagers on the beach, lifting their voices in song to the Gods and remembering their glorious ancestors. Nani chanted behind the Chief as he bowed to the sea and prayed for a safe journey. The sun was glorious upon the horizon.

Thousands of crabs scampered over the sand and into the ocean. The sun emerged to see the spectacle as they streamed around the Chief on the beach before he arose and walked into the waves to launch offerings for the next stage. As Nani chanted behind the Chief, a pod of dolphins appeared in the bay, lifting the hearts of the voyagers. They felt blessed by the sea and its majestic creatures.

They hailed the arrival of the dolphins as an auspicious omen. Dolphins had guided them to the island, and they would commence the next phase of the journey in a positive frame of mind. They thanked and praised Earth Mother, the island's guardians, for the hospitable welcome, fresh water, and food. They laid a carving in the bay to tell the story of their voyage.

At last, the canoes were ready to launch, and the voyager's feet left the land again for life on the open sea until they found a place to settle. The sails were hoisted, and people settled into their places on the canoe, watching the island diminish behind them. But this time, without the angst of leaving behind friends, family and their homes.

Starman and Nani said they would sail past other islands in the group. The Chief decided there was nothing to be gained from going ashore again as the resupplying of the canoes was more than sufficient.

Marama sat at the rear of the canoe, her hair lifting in the stiff breeze, watching Starman setting the course with the newly balanced paddles. He was in deep conversation with the other navigators.

The injured bird sat beside her, lifting his beak into the wind. While it was much recovered, he could still not fly, and the Chief and Nani suggested they take the bird with them. If it recovered, it would fly south, and that was where they were going.

Marama and Starman loved the idea nearly as much as the children, who, after much debating, had settled on naming him Manu (bird). She stroked Manu's feathers absentmindedly as she faced the open sea, feeling the exhilaration and freedom of being a voyager, another creature of the ocean and the baby seemed to be revelling in the constant motion. Marama sincerely hoped she would be spared from the morning sickness many expectant mothers experienced. She had a good supply of herbs to quell any nausea. Starman looked at her with a beaming smile. He was definitely in his element, almost childlike in his enthusiasm for his craft. Love for him swelled in her chest, almost painful in its intensity. She looked ahead as tears pricked behind her eyes from the well of emotion. Marama chastised herself for being a sentimental fool. The bird blinked at her, opening his beak in a laugh.

"Don't you go telling any tales, Manu," she told the bird. He closed his beak tight and tucked it into his chest.

The sailing was good, the currents and winds favourable. They could not have hoped for a better start to the voyage. Dolphins escorted them out of the bay and played around the canoes while the voyagers squealed at their antics. The other islands in the group slid past the canoes as they navigated their chosen course, and the rhythm of life settled.

The replenishing of food meant they had a wide variety of things to eat and drink on the first part of the journey, which tended to keep people in a good mood. Every day, Nani was occupied with following the instructions of her ancestors, and Marama spent time learning the nuances of tending to the spiritual world. The old woman's memory was astounding, and Marama despaired of retaining and recalling the many chants and rituals required. But she practised in the evening, and when performing other tasks, she recited the words in her head repeatedly, visualising herself completing the subtle movements, a different language, that Nani used with the spirit world. Marama tried to balance her duties, studies, and helping Nani with attending Starman and being a good woman.

It was all new to her, and she was not entirely sure how she was doing, so Marama pushed herself hard. Starman was a self-sufficient man, she realised, used to caring for himself. Marama wondered if she was a failure as his woman, but he seemed happy, so perhaps she was overthinking. Deciding to speak to Ari, Marama would ask her what she should be doing for her man. Ari was the head woman of a busy household for the Chief and had more experience.

In the evenings, Marama and the baby treasured her stargazing lessons with Starman. Since the exchange between the baby and his ancestors, her ability to find stars and constellations and to comprehend the map they formed had improved.

It was also a time of privacy for the couple in the early morning hours when everyone else was sleeping. They held each other, shared dreams and generally enjoyed their newfound romance. When Starman set the course, he woke another navigator for his shift, and he and Marama retired together. Snuggling against one another, they tried not to awaken anyone else.

Neither seemed to be getting much sleep, but they were shining with health, faces lit from inside by their growing love.

Everything went well until the fourth night at sea. They had not been asleep for long when Starman's eyes flew open, and Marama jolted awake beside him.

"The wind has changed, and something is amiss," he whispered.

He immediately headed towards the navigator, who was sleeping soundly and did not awaken when shaken. Marama and Nani were beside him. The night was dark, with thick clouds obscuring the stars and the wind whipped in swirling gusts.

"My spirit guide awakened me. They have been unable to breach the defences we put in place, so they turn their ill intent to the elements to cause us harm. Marama, can you get the Chief? We need his strength and some decisions," she said, voice deadly as an obsidian blade. Marama did not get far as the Chief was headed for them, and they collided in the dark. Marama whispered that something was wrong. Starman had seized the paddle, steadying the canoe drifting at the mercy of the wind and waves.

"We cannot wake him, Chief. This is no ordinary sleep but an enchantment placed upon a vulnerable man while we were busy elsewhere. I have made many offerings to the wind, but it's been angered by malevolent spirits. I must find a way to counteract this, Chief. I will need you," Nani said.

"Nani, I will join you too. We are strongest when we are together," said Marama.

"Marama, it's you they seek. You may draw more enemies towards us in the next realm. At this time, you are a liability rather than a strength," she said, shaking her head.

The Chief nodded his agreement. He did not want to place Marama and the baby in harm's way again. Nani deserved his support. Marama's tense body announced her disagreement. She did not argue, just looked at the Chief forlornly in the dark, hoping he might change his mind.

Nani took Chief's hand, pulling him to sit beside her. She wasted no time entering the spirit world and linking with her guide.

Marama felt her way towards Starman, who was wrestling with the paddle and steering as the wind and turbulent waves continued their discordant motion.

"I am surprised nobody else is awake, especially the navigators. The canoe is being battered and rocked constantly," said Starman.

"Nani said the sleep is an enchantment. The four of us have protections woven to shield us from evil spirits, so we are immune to the effects. What can I do to assist you?" Marama asked.

"I need to put us back on course, Marama. No stars are in sight, and I have no idea how long we drifted or in what direction we move. I must listen to my sea father and call on my ancestor." He clutched the pounamu pendant. "I trust my directional instincts, but to do that,

I must block out the chaos surrounding us. Can you chant and sing close to me to help me focus?" he asked.

Marama nodded and squeezed his hand. She closed her eyes and clasped Starman's leg, feeling his muscles flexing and tightening as he tried to steady the canoe. An ancient chant came to mind about how a voyager played his flute to calm the sea, seduce the wind and win a passage through a storm. Nani taught it to her as a child. As she sang, she laid her face against Starman's back so the rhythm of her breathing merged with his body. He closed his eyes to better feel the motion of the waves and the direction of the wind as it slapped his face relentlessly.

Starman followed his ancestor. He sensed a pattern in the waves, the direction of the current flowing underneath the choppy waves, and guided the canoe to follow that current to the southern oceans. Marama synchronised the beating of their hearts, the cadence of her chant, the bursts of joy from the baby, Starman's body moving and underpinning it all was the movement in the deep.

A vision burst behind her eyes of a giant colourful fish swimming lazily underneath their canoe, and the baby connected with his grandfather. Streaming impulses to his father through her touch, Marama sighed, content.

A shark flashed across her vision. She shouted a warning to grandfather, but he had dived to avoid the enormous predator marauding beneath the canoe, menacing and looking for her.

An unfathomable well of hate for Marama emanated from the shark. It turned cold black eyes towards her. Stalking her, an apex predator of old. Marama chanted on, blocking out the vision. She was in the physical world, and she was not prey. She sang of the battle of their village, of Piki slaying the scout, of Tane deflecting the spear, turning the outcome of the battle and finally, of her vengeance.

Tane's presence swirled around them as the shark rammed the canoe, venting its fury against the hardwood. Marama started as a second shark of unbelievable size swooped in. It tore into the shark that had stunned itself against the waka. Tane shared his satisfaction with Marama as he exacted revenge on his killer.

Marama heard Nani gasp behind her. She shook her head to clear the gory spectacle and felt her way to Nani's side. The Chief held Nani upright, his body streaming with sweat, his breath rasping as if he'd been running, and the old woman trembled with exhaustion. Marama found water and placed an arm around Nani to support her from the other side so she could take a sip.

"Nani, what can I do?" she asked, handing the water to the thirsty Chief. Nani patted her hand and leaned on Marama. Searching around her, Maram knew the navigators kept a weather cloak handy. She found it and threw it around Nani's shoulders.

"Do you need anything, Chief? she asked. He squeezed her arm and shook his head, still too tired to speak. That galvanised Marama. She reached into her medicine pouch and found the packet with tiny cakes of pulverised seeds and herbs baked hard with honey. Removing two and placing one in Nani's mouth, she passed the other to the Chief. The cakes were for reviving people with low energy reserves in stressed bodies. Marama hoped they would work.

The sea had calmed, and the wind dropped like it never blew ill. Starman came to check what had happened. He felt Marama's surprise in the tension of her body and heard Nani's gasp behind him. At that point, Starman dared not let go of the paddle as the current called him to follow. The Chief recovered his breath, thanked Marama and told them he would be fine. They were in a battle unlike any other. Nani would have to explain what occurred because he did not understand it.

Reassured Chief was well, Starman returned to the navigation as everyone else slept soundly. The night was still dark, so Starman lit the beacon as he had no idea where the other canoe was. Or if the others had remained on course while their canoe drifted on the ocean.

Far ahead in the distance, he spotted a twinkling light as the navigator in the second canoe lit a beacon in response.

They had separated in the swirling winds to avoid a collision and were relieved they found each other. One benefit of the darkness was the beacons burned brightly in the gloom. Still, with no stars or moon, he was unsure where they were in relation to the course he set. However, they travelled on the southern current.

Starman hoped the morning would bring a fine sunrise to give them an accurate easterly bearing. The sleepy navigator allowed the waka to drift in a westerly direction.

He paused momentarily, head bowed, to thank his sea father and ancestors for finding the southern current. Blowing off course could have taken them out of the winds and currents they needed to reach their destination. Other voyagers told of endless days without wind, becalmed in the middle of the ocean. With this many passengers, that was not a fate they could afford to experience.

Nani patted Marama's hand with more vigour as she recovered some strength. She wasn't sure where to begin but felt like she could speak and tell Marama what happened. Her guide came to her immediately and surrounded her with their ancestors to protect her from the gloom and sleep the enemy ancestors created in the spiritual world to throw over the canoe.

Their ancestors whispered that the enemy spirits told the wind the voyagers only worshipped the God of the Sea and cared nothing for the other elements or the stars, that they were arrogant and disrespectful to the other Gods. Nani must appease the angry wind by reminding it of the offerings and invocations made to all. Nani began her entreaty to the wind God, the clouds, the stars, but the spiteful spirits whispered all at once to drown out her voice. Even though mortal voices were much louder in their world, she was told to join her voice with that of the Chief. So Nani pulled the Chief to the edge of the spirit world and asked him to lend her his voice.

It worked, and Nani shouted of their offerings and prayers before and during the journey. But the spirits tried everything to block the sound from reaching the wind. They placed themselves in the way and created whirlwinds to push her words in the wrong direction.

The Chief hoisted Nani on his shoulders so her voice would project over the obstacles, and he ran from side to side to make it harder to block the sound. Chief also summoned his ancestors to aid them and carry their words to the wind and the stars. Together, they strived to push back the gloom sent against them. Slowly, it retreated. The ancestors were muttering and angry but did not want to detract from the stories unfolding, meant for the ears of the Gods.

Nani had a burst of inspiration and called on Starman's grandfather, who told of the exceptional child created by Tane, the stargazer son of the sea and Marama, who was born under and named after the light of the moon. The elements and Gods were enlightened on how Marama and the unborn child joined Nani in worship. And the Chief, who lent her his voice to bare the lies woven by vengeful spirits. Nani threw all her strength behind this tale, drawing on the Chief to expose the lies and how wrongly they were punished.

The effort drained them mentally, spiritually and physically. By now, Nani knew she must retreat before she over-taxed herself and the Chief, who had never been in the spirit world.

A frightening roar of the wind silenced the muttering spirits, dissipating in an angry gale. Stars burst in the gloom, and waves thundered, sweeping them away with a hiss.

"Who dares to claim a child of mine with lies or to use one of my creatures for their own purpose?" boomed an angry presence. Not exactly a voice, more like the reverberation of a thousand crashing waves in the distance. They retreated from the realm of spirits.

With their ancestors' help, they succeeded in making themselves heard. Retribution was swift. The Gods did not like to be lied to or used against those who honoured and revered them. As Nani slumped into her depleted body, she experienced the jolt of the mad shark hitting the canoe. It was possessed by the poisonous spirit of Mako before it was torn to shreds and devoured by Tane, who was aided by the angry God of the Sea.

Marama explained the chanting, Starman finding the rhythm of the ocean, the underlying southern current and visions of grandfather fish. The malevolence of the shark stalking her and the swift and bloody end it met.

"This is good news, Marama. You are free from the enemy in life and death. The God of the Sea is also claiming the unborn child. The baby's presence infiltrates two realms. My little grandson, and now I must rest," she smiled.

The child pulsed warmth inside Marama, basking in Nani's praise. She stroked her belly unconsciously in a soothing response. Relief that the threat was dispelled fluttered with the motion of her hands.

Chief enfolded her in his arms, and as her face met the comforting warmth of his shoulder, Marama's tears came. He patted her hair as he had done with his children, letting her release the pent-up emotions pushed aside to cope with the attack.

Finally, she lifted her head and wiped her eyes, but the Chief kept a comforting arm around her. She had been just another child playing in the village a few months ago. Although she was highly competent, Marama was young.

"Tane always looked upon you as his father. I feel the same way. Thank you for always being here for me, even when I blubber like a baby," she smiled.

"Ari and I regard you as our daughter. Tane was not my biological son, but he was the one most like me," he said.

"You must be exhausted too, Chief. Please go and rest. I will sit with Starman until one of the other navigators is awake and watch Nani. She is slow to recover. I have calmed myself. You make me feel better. I suddenly felt overwhelmed by everything."

The Chief squeezed her shoulder and kissed her forehead before heading toward the allure of Ari's body warmth and the healing embrace of sleep. Marama positioned herself behind Starman again, her head upon his back and arms around his waist.

"I am not interfering with your work, am I?" she asked.

"No, I am tired. Your company is just what I need," Starman said, reaching behind to pull Marama closer. "Besides, apart from following the current south and heading towards the other waka, I am not navigating us anywhere in the dark. I am going to take a break. I can think of something better to do," he said huskily.

Marama clung to him, returning his kisses fervently. Maybe it was the aftermath of the storm and battle. They were acutely aware of how close they came to losing their way and each other, which translated into a desperate need for each other physically.

"Everybody else is still sleeping. The night is pitch dark. We should make the most of it," Marama breathed in his ear as she threw the weather cloak around his shoulders and climbed onto his lap, back to the ocean, so if anyone did wake up, they wouldn't see anything.

"You are a wicked woman. No wonder I love you," he whispered as they coupled and brought their bodies to a shuddering, intense ecstasy. It was as if the danger they lived through had magnified their senses. They held each other as long as they dared, feeling the lethargy creep into tired limbs as they slumped together. Marama reluctantly tore herself from Starman's body to wash, and she thought she saw the sleeping navigator turn over in his sleep.

"We are both exhausted. I am going to try and rouse the navigator. Then we sneak off to bed so he isn't embarrassed that he fell asleep. You need to sleep, too. Come as soon as you can. I need you," she said, placing her palm on his cheek.

Marama took a sewing needle from her pouch, placed the sharp point against the sleeping navigator's big toe, and slowly applied pressure until his foot twitched and jerked away. She did the same on the other side, knowing the pain would send warning signals throughout his body. Repositioning herself behind his head, she squeezed his earlobes, gently at first but more firmly until his head moved from side to side, trying to avoid the pain. She melted into the dark as his eyelids began to flutter. Starman washed himself, needing the cold water to revive him as his body craved rest. He wanted to crawl onto his mat beside Marama.

Starman sprinkled cold water on the navigator, who was stirring now, struggling to escape the effects of the enchantment. The navigator sat up with a start, blinking his eyes, then rubbing them in disbelief as he looked around and saw Starman still steering the canoe.

"Starman, did I fall asleep on my watch?" he asked incredulously.

"Yes, my friend, along with almost everyone except Marama and me. Please forgive me for not waking you. The opportunity to be alone with my new woman overwhelmed me," he grinned.

"But you have been navigating three shifts out of four, Starman. I have never fallen asleep on my watch before. I am so sorry. Please forgive my laziness and go get some sleep," he stammered.

"I won't say no to more time with Marama, but seriously, I did not need to wake you. You were right here all night. The night is dark, and there are no stars. I am merely steering us towards the beacon on the other waka as the winds separated us in the gloom. I need you to look for the sun and find the easterly reference point. We are in the stream of the southern current and need to re-plot our course when the stars are visible," he said.

As casually as possible, Starman strode off to his sleeping place. The navigator would know they had blown off course, but Starman hoped he wasn't burdened with guilt. The Chief and Nani hadn't mentioned whether they wished to keep the battle of the spirits to themselves or if they would tell everyone. It wasn't his place to decide. Marama reached for him as Starman lay beside her. They snuggled together as had become their habit, so they were connected in sleep. And sleep, they did. Mental and physical fatigue claimed them while Manu watched over them, blinking and preening his feathers.

Chapter 11

A cloudy, damp day greeted the groggy voyagers, who woke feeling like they had participated in a night of feasting. The navigator briefed his colleagues on the plan for the day and reiterated Starman's instructions. They now had a line of sight to the other canoe and would rendezvous this morning.

Everyone went about their business. The only surprise was that the Chief and Nani slept until late morning, which was unusual. Starman and Marama were often up during the night, so nobody thought anything of them sleeping most of the day.

Only Ari's intuition sensed something odd had happened during the night. Nobody complained about their child waking up or the wind or sea being noisy like usual, and neither the Chief nor Nani were late risers. Ari was a light sleeper, but nothing disturbed her all night. She did not mention her suspicions to anyone. It was better to wait for her man to awaken and tell her what had occurred while she slept like a baby.

To Ari's surprise, it was noon before the Chief or Nani surfaced. She took them food and drink as Marama still slept. As the Chief ate his food hungrily, she threw him a look that conveyed all the questions she wanted to ask, but he looked exhausted.

Nani joined them so she wouldn't rouse Starman and Marama. Ari noticed Nani's face was drawn. The old woman looked weak, so she added dried fruit pulp to her drink. Nani was grateful, nodding her thanks and ate just as the Chief did. So Ari sat patiently. If there was something to tell that she should know, they would inform her.

At last, the Chief finished, thanked and hugged her as she stooped to retrieve the bowl. His look conveyed how much he loved her, which made her heart skip beats still after all the years together. Ari cleared Nani's bowl, replenished their drinks and brought some fruit. Somehow, they both seemed depleted.

"Please sit with us, Ari. I know you noticed last night was no ordinary night," said the Chief. He came quickly to the point, as was his way. They shared with Ari the trials of the night. The sleep enchantment, the elemental fury, their venture into the spiritual world, Marama's vision, Starman's communion with the sea, the mad shark and its demise.

They watched her reaction as the story unfolded and saw her emotional dilemma as she looked from one to another, hanging on every word. At the tale's end, she burst into tears and threw her arms around the Chief's neck, holding him close.

"I am sorry," she sobbed through her tears, "I can't bear the thought of losing you, and I couldn't help at all. I just slept through the whole thing," she cried.

"My child, nobody could have helped us where we travelled last night. We would not have risked anybody else; even Marama, a trained spirit walker, was refused this task. Do not be so hard on yourself; please know our Chief still holds much power. We are exhausted, but we won a great victory," she said.

Ari dried her eyes but stayed in her man's arms, wanting to be close to reassure herself he was fine.

"Nani, I think there is merit in sharing what happened with everyone. Possibly, there are benefits in shielding them from the truth, but I am inclined to be honest. What do you think?" he asked.

"I tend to agree, Chief. We are on this journey together. It is better not to keep secrets on a canoe. Our victory has liberated us from a threat, a positive outcome. It would be good to include everyone in a ceremony of thanks," she concluded.

The Chief decided to wait until Starman and Marama were awake, then bring the two waka to a meeting and tell the whole tale of the night they all missed.

"Now, Ari, I regret to advise you I am hungry again. I don't know how Nani copes with her spirit walking because I feel I burned all my reserves and could eat a whale for lunch by myself," he said, grinning. Ari laughed and kissed him before heading to find more food.

Marama and Starman finally awoke, and they were also ravenous. The children had already overfed Manu, and he was perched on the side of the canoe, watching them play.

After yawning, stretching and dousing their faces with cold seawater, Starman and Marama found the Chief, Nani and Ari. Prepared this time, Ari made a massive meal of smoked birds, salted fish, taro, raw fish, dried coconut cakes, fruit and sweet tea. To her surprise, the Chief and Nani ate again, so she teased them that parasites had invaded their pukus. That set the mood for the meal, degenerating into a competition of making fun of their hearty appetites.

Marama was supposed to be eating for two, not three or four. Starman's tall stature was blamed on growing to accommodate his stomach in his legs and torso. It was an entertaining meal, filled with good food and light-hearted banter between family. After the strain of the previous night, it was welcome.

After they ate, the Chief shared his plans for the meeting and asked each of them if they would share their part in last night's events. He wanted to include everyone in the tale, allow them to share the victory and make songs or retell the story as part of their voyage and history. Nani nodded her agreement. They should be proud of making this journey and overcoming the obstacles.

The Chief called the meeting, and Ari introduced the story by speaking of her misgivings in the morning and her intuition that all was not as it should be.

As she recounted the unusual events she had noticed, people nodded or scratched their heads, thinking of things they recalled once focused. Then Starman told of waking due to the chaotic motion of the canoe. Nani spoke of her spirit guide, alerting her and finding people in an enchanted sleep.

The Chief recounted his premonition that his people needed him and that something was amiss. The players retold the whole story, each giving as much detail and emotion to the telling as they could. All the voyagers were transfixed as the tale unfolded. They gasped when Marama spoke of the hunting shark and covered their mouths in horror. Eyes widened when Nani and the Chief told of the battle of words in the spirit realm. When the tale ended, they were silent.

Then they gave a mighty cheer and shook their fists in victory before giving thanks to all the Gods and ancestors they could. The Chief suggested Nani lead them in communal thanks for their deliverance from harm, and everybody was enthusiastic about doing so. Men, women and children chanted and sang passionately, grateful to be safe.

Marama looked to the sky and saw a flock of birds in the distance. She remembered the words of the spirit. As the birds drew nearer, Manu shook out and flapped his wings, slowly lifting into the air and hovering above the waka. He screeched a farewell. Now free of the splint, his mended leg no longer troubled him. The wings were beautiful with perfectly groomed feathers as he wheeled in circles above them, going higher and higher to join the migrating formation of his kind.

"The birds migrate to the southern land, so we have a new course," shouted Starman. He was already running to the paddle to make the adjustments.

"We are truly blessed by the Gods and ancestors on this journey. Our thanks have been rewarded," cried Nani.

"Everyone to their places. We sail and follow the birds to our new home," shouted the Chief.

"Goodbye, Manu," whispered Marama. "May you have a long and good life. You have fulfilled an important purpose and I hope we meet again."

The voyager's hopes lifted with the friendly wind filling their sails. It was almost as if the wind God tried to make amends on the new course.

Even the falling rain was a boon as it replenished their fresh water supplies for washing. They set up the rain capture devices they had brought with them. The dried skins were sewn together to form a funnel to catch the rainwater and direct it into storage vessels. While the water inevitably tasted salty, with so many people on board, it was good to refill emptied vessels.

People busied themselves with the daily chores, and the Chief continued his lessons. Nani and the Chief set the youngsters a competition to come up with the best artistic representation of their voyage so far and gave them three days to rehearse.

The clouds cleared when the sun sank on the second day of following the birds' course. Starman and Marama looked forward to seeing their beloved stars when darkness descended. There would also be a moon tonight, and Marama spent the day planning a ritual to thank her namesake.

As grateful as Starman was for Manu and the birds showing them the way, it was his nature to check and check again when it came to their course. The winds could be fickle at this time of the year, and he did not want to take them too far south.

Tonight, everyone would gather for a communal meal. Afterwards, some of the adults, the best storytellers, would entertain the children with amusing tales that offered moral lessons.

This plan pleased their parents, who would have some leisure time. The navigation team invited anyone up late to join them when Starman checked and adjusted the course, if necessary, by the moon and stars. There was quite a turnout, even though the early morning hours provided the best visibility of the constellations Starman needed. The Chief, Ari, the grandson who should have been asleep, and Nani took seats as the navigator began his position checks.

Starman was endlessly patient, pointing out the groups of stars, their names, their position in the current season, the phase of the moon, and where they sat relative to the east and west. Some of his calculations applying the direction of the wind and current were complicated. Still, he managed to simplify them enough for everyone to follow the gist of what he was doing.

He invited Marama to show everyone the calculations she did each night to figure out where they had come from, reassuring everyone there was always a path home if they or future generations were inclined to return. Each navigator took a few people interested in the stars and gave them a lesson, some stories and generally fanned any flames of interest.

In the end, the birds flew true in their arrow formation, and only a few minor corrections were necessary due to the waka wanting to make landfall further north than the birds.

As people drifted off, Marama and Starman remained awake, enjoying the freshness of the cool night air and the normality of the evening. Marama sat cross-legged in meditation, beginning her ritual of thanks to the moon. She felt the tang of the air in her expanding lungs, the silvery light of the moon behind her eyelids and her mind expanding beyond the boundaries of her body.

"You are welcome, Marama. We will have a child. I also claim him as my mokopuna. He reaches for me even now," laughed the moon, her celestial voice mercurial, tinkling and shiny.

"My love, you are almost there," whispered Tane. It was as if he spoke from a great distance now. "I will always love and watch over you both, but I must relinquish you to live your mortal life without interference or tinged with sadness."

Then he was gone. But this time, there was a finality to his farewell. For a moment, Marama felt bereft as the loss of Tane crashed over her like waves breaking on the reef, running into thousands of rivulets, momentum and beauty shattered by the impact. Tane had been part of her life for as long as she could remember. Her first love, and now part of her heart, was fading, dying, severed brutally from the rest. Marama pulsed with pain as the moon washed her in its light. Nani came to her side, feeling her angst.

"Marama, you have to let Tane go. He exists in another realm. He has helped you find new love, hope and a shared dream through the child. This has cost him dearly. He needs the peaceful sanctuary of the next world to wash away the sorrows of his loss in this one," Nani murmured. She held Marama against her breast and closed her eyes. The baby was worried. He acknowledged the pain but didn't understand and pulsated confusion through them. Marama stroked her belly to calm him, reassuring the baby she was hurt and sad because his spirit father had left her.

"Go to Starman, my child. You must seek comfort and let your love flourish without any reservations. This is vital to the happiness of the three of you as a family. That is why Tane came to say goodbye."

Nani kissed her gently, then returned to bed, leaving Marama alone to regain her composure. She knew Nani and Tane were right. Starman was a wonderful man, and she loved him dearly. Marama also knew a part of her would always belong to her first love.

"I will always love you, Tane," she whispered to the night.

Starman held his arm out when he heard Marama approaching and stroked her face when he saw she was troubled and had been crying. He kissed her forehead and eyes, searching her face for the source of misery. She hugged him fiercely, crushing the wind out of him with the strength of her arms. Starman just held her, trying to comfort her. If she wanted to tell him what bothered her, she would do so in her own time.

"Promise me you will never leave me in this life," she said vehemently. Starman promised, even though they both knew they would not live forever. It was what Marama needed to hear today, so he promised, guessing the source of her grief. Tane loved her enough to watch over Marama after he was killed, and Starman had experienced her love and passion for Tane first-hand. Perhaps Marama would love him like that one day, given some time.

The navigator had never been in love before but was beginning to understand how intense it was. Marama ignited more than just his passion. The tenderness continued to surprise him. The pair were united by more than just the baby. Marama chose Starman for herself, which comforted him, for he couldn't compete with a memory. They sat together in companionable silence until the shift navigator arrived for his briefing, leaving Starman to retire. Holding Marama as she succumbed to sleep, Starman helped her let go of the turbulence inside.

The next day was sunny. People hummed as they worked on tasks for the day. The breeze was warm and invited good moods. Children sunned themselves when they could escape chores or lessons. Most were enjoying the voyage as the biggest adventure of their short lives. The adaptability of children was often underestimated by less flexible adults. Nani planned a busy program for her and Marama to keep the young woman's mind occupied. Marama had known so much loss, grief, and pain in her life, but Nani knew there was much to look forward to in future. She would build a life and family in the new land. Nani hoped she would be there to share some of that life with them and decided to stretch her old limbs. Nani couldn't afford to become decrepit just yet.

A golden day of voyaging on the open sea slid by as the canoes skimmed the water with the grace and beauty that mirrored the sailing sun across the sky. The navigators had stirred enthusiasm during the voyage and often found themselves supervising during the day.

The Chief began exercising his warriors, refreshing skills and stretching unused muscles while the weather was accommodating. Starman and the navigation team worked with the warriors while the youngsters took charge of the waka.

It felt good to breathe hard, sweat and renew their acquaintance with their weapons. Many striking weapons had names or stories associated with them, and some had been part of a family for many generations. The Chief honed his whalebone club to perfection through hours of attention to the striking surface and talking it to it as a friend. Ari often told him she was jealous that he shared more caresses with his weapon than her. Even though the comments were made in jest, there was some truth to them. The weapon became an extension of Chief in battle, saving his life or winning the day on countless occasions. This weapon was called The Protector and would be handed to the next Chief after he stepped down, rather than staying in one particular family.

Nani gifted Starman a fine collection of weapons from her family to be handed down to the child, and any other sons he and Marama might have.

It was prudent he practised as they did not know who they would encounter in the new land or what kind of welcome to expect. Familiarity and confidence in your weapons could mean the difference between life and death in battle. Any voyagers who journeyed south would likely be hardy but not necessarily friendly. The Chief and his key advisors decided they would not land immediately when they arrived but scout the area along the coastline and find somewhere safe to go ashore.

The days became longer, so they made the most of the golden twilight and the warmth before evening closed in. The fishing was excellent. They could not believe the size of the fish they caught. Daily contests were held for boasting rights on who caught the best tuna or snapper.

Each day, the first fish caught, sometimes the largest as well, was returned to the sea to thank the sea God for his bounty and favour.

As they travelled southeast, the weather was changeable, and the waves tossed them about. Every day, they knew their destination was closer. Marama mended her broken heart by throwing herself into her spiritual studies with Nani, navigating with Starman and lavishing her family with love.

Life was stirring within her, so she spent the evenings with Ari discussing what to prepare and what she should expect. Ari was a stellar source of information, and it was one less task for Nani. Maram checked on the baby she delivered often, talked to her mother and enjoyed playing and cuddling the baby girl.

Marama worried about the effects of the damp, salty air on Nani. Still, the old woman seemed more energetic and sprightly than ever. It appeared that adventure agreed with her. The schedule of rituals and offerings the ancestors suggested was demanding. Marama felt she learned at an accelerated rate, and she completed several ceremonies without Nani. She wanted to do this to take the workload from Nani. She was proud that Starman joined the Chief's close circle of advisors with a natural ease that required no discussion, meaning the Chief had more support.

There would be many challenges when they reached the new land. Starman advised them one of his ancestors had returned and told them that no coconuts existed in the southern land. It was a shock to many who could not imagine life without coconuts.

Coconuts provided food, drink, fibre, shelter, bowls, and wood. They wondered how they would cope without all those things. Nani and Starman explained the southern lands were always described as bountiful. Rich in wood, seafood, birdlife, hunting, and fish in rivers and lakes as well as the sea, fertile soil and the land was much larger than the islands. These descriptions helped assuage fears and created a sense of excitement around what they would discover.

The carvers listened to the tales of giant trees that lived for generations, and their fingers twitched at the thought of all the beautiful items they might create. Women dreamed of bathing in fresh, clear water again, finding delicious food, making new homes, growing vegetables and being on land again where their children could entertain themselves.

Marama lay down to sleep, and Starman curled around her, cocooning his little family with his body. She felt herself step into the dream.

Starman's grandfather was sitting on a rock in the middle of a coral cay, beckoning her to join him, then motioning her to sit when she materialised at his side. They watched the waves lap the shore for a moment, appreciating the dazzling azure of the ocean over the white sand. Grandfather took Marama's hand and held it to his lips.

"You and Tane have made Starman, me and our ancestors happy, Marama. The baby will restore our line for generations to come, and the God of the sea will be served by worthy sons. He must return to the sea cave of my home with his father. You will not want to let them go, but you must, my dear. When they depart, you will carry another son who will not survive the journey. However, these are events of the future, not why I invited you into this dream. You approach the southern land, your destination. We are sending you a guide to lead you to your new home. Do not land anywhere else, or you risk confrontation. Watch for the guide. It is bonded to the baby for life," he said. Smiling and evaporating, he left Marama to her much-needed sleep.

When Marama awoke, she remembered the dream. She replayed it and went to Nani before she forgot anything. They decided to share the dream with the Chief and Starman, so Marama woke the navigator while Nani sought the Chief.

As Marama recounted the dream, Chief nodded as if in agreement. He was concerned about landing in other people's territory as they might be perceived as hostile.

Starman looked at her in wonder. He couldn't believe she had communicated with his beloved grandfather. Starman had already dreamed of returning to the sea cave to initiate his unborn son, and there would also be another son.

Nani looked thoughtful but pleased. Her guide had sent a vision of where to locate the new village. How it should look, including many details she must discuss with the Chief. The Chief and Nani found time in their schedules to discuss what Nani had seen.

Marama and Starman left hand in hand to find food and spend time together while at leisure. She could feel the buoyancy of his mood. The dream filled him with joy. Her only misgiving was knowing one day, he and their son would leave her.

However, the guide to show them where to settle, Nani's vision of where to build the village, and the fact that their relationship would last and produce more children were all positive tidings. Marama decided not to dwell on what she could not control.

Marama loved hearing about Starman's childhood, his village, his family and customs. For his part, Starman wanted to know her, what she liked and disliked, how she thought and looked at the world. Although they were expecting a child, they were also getting to know one another better.

They laughed at their back-to-front relationship and were affectionate with each other, which meant lots of teasing. Still, it did not stop them. As they cuddled to-gether at the front of the canoe, staring at the ocean, banks of beautiful clouds stretched on the horizon.

"Marama, I think that is land ahead," said Starman squinting. "Aotearoa, land of the long white cloud, we have found you."

The excitement spread like wildfire through the canoe as people strained to see. They couldn't actually see the

land, but the clouds clustered around a huge island, and
they trusted Starman and the navigators, who were sure
they had found a significant land mass.

Chapter 12

When the guide arrived, he announced his presence in a spectacular fashion. Breaching the waves and slapping his enormous tail was a whale.

He wanted them to follow him, and he put on a show. Swam away, then came back to check they were with him, breaching frequently to remain visible.

The baby's excitement welled inside Marama. This was his guide, a lifelong bonded companion grandfather had said.

"You don't do things in a small way, do you, little man?" she asked.

"We all have a guide, Marama. His is just the largest one I have ever seen."

"What is your guide?"

Starman showed her the stylised moray eel featured in the flowing tā moko on his arms, his guide. It had been his guide they had returned to the sea in the ceremony of thanks when he was welcomed into their midst; it all made sense to Marama.

The whale stayed out to sea, and they followed behind him, feeling privileged to be guided to their new home by such a majestic creature.

As the whale could travel at tremendous speed, he often wallowed playfully, waiting for them and captivating everyone on board. They were awed by its immense size and strength.

When the whale slapped its tail in the distance, it sent magnificent water sprays into the air. It was an incomparable sight to behold. At last, the whale changed course and swam toward the mass of clouds where they would find land. The canoes made the course adjustment to stay with their guide. Everyone was at the sides of the waka, waiting to catch a glimpse of land, their new home and hoping that the landing would go smoothly.

Nani had been fasting. This aided her in her forays into the spirit realm and allowed her to maintain the connection for a longer time. Her spirit guide showed her many valuable resources and designs that would assist them in surviving and thriving in the new home. When the guide arrived, she took a journey to inspect the location of the new village from above and take bearings to help her find the correct spot.

The ancestors chose a new home for them. Somewhere, their descendants would be safe and could remember them. It was a new home for the people and a spiritual home for the ancestors.

Nani flew free of her body, soaring above the ocean until she came to rest on top of a hill wreathed in mist. Her ancestors surrounded her, whispering that this would be their home. From the hilltop, she saw a sheltered bay in the distance and below her a plateau about two-thirds of the way up the hill, with a spring-fed stream running down the left-hand side. The ancestors told her they would send a dream to the Chief; the hill village needed to be fortified so it could be easily defended in the future. They showed Nani the best places to grow crops and revealed the bounty of the fertile forests as they winged back towards the canoe.

When Nani opened her eyes, she found Marama sitting in front of her with a restorative drink, and she smiled her thanks.

"My guide, old grandfather, told me you would journey to our new home spiritually before we arrived. I sensed you return just now," said Marama.

Nani nodded, sipped her drink and was extremely pleased that Marama had progressed rapidly in her spiritual lessons. She was unaware Marama was cognisant of her entering and exiting the next realm.

"I now know exactly how to find the location from the landing place. The ancestors have chosen well," said Nani.

Emotion crackled in her voice. She recounted her experience to Marama, recalling every minute detail she could as each one was significant to their survival in the future.

Marama hugged Nani to her as they returned to watching the directions of their guide. They were sure he was leading them to the vicinity of the sheltered bay where their village would be built above. Marama was having a strange experience. The unborn child was jubilant, and Marama was having flashes of vision as if she was riding upon the whale's back both above and under the water. This amused Nani greatly, and she chuckled as she patted Marama's belly, making little clucking noises. It appeared Marama's disciplinarian would be the proudest, most indulgent great-grandmother of all time. Rolling her eyes heavenwards, Marama lamented that was not what she needed to anyone listening.

"This is all your fault, Tane. Don't think you can run off and leave me to deal with these two. I know you can hear me even if you are not talking back," she scolded inside her head. That made her feel much better. Nani always said a problem shared is a problem halved, and Tane deserved at least a third of the issues.

Slowly, they closed in on the land. Now, they saw the coastline looming endless and green in the distance. It called to them this land. The waves sang of the future, the generations of people who would be born and die here, their bones becoming part of the land until the two became indistinguishable.

The whale led them on, never faltering in his task, ensuring they could see him and kept following. An ethereal mist descended, cloaking them as the evening approached. They could no longer see the land, but they were also invisible to anyone looking seaward from land. Their arrival was inconspicuous and went unnoticed.

The mist lifted as abruptly as it had descended, and in the fading light, the whale led them into the bay in the calm of evening. The forest that grew to the edge of a sandy bay was lush and green. Towering trees, some sprouting bright red flowers, the colour of leadership, fringed the bay in a spectacular welcome. The flowers had bloomed where they stopped to replenish their supplies, so there was a warm familiarity.

Tears sprang to the eyes of many of the voyagers as they finally looked upon the land they had travelled so far to find. People hugged one another in joy and relief, weeping openly.

The whale turned and waved its flippers in farewell before returning to the deep as the voyagers blew it kisses and called their thanks to an excellent guide. It was a memory they would always treasure, and soon, it would become a scene immortalised in works of art in many forms as they recorded the history of founding the new village.

"Nani, is it safe to go ashore, or should I send a scouting party?" asked the Chief.

"It is safe, my Chief. I scouted the landing place with the ancestors. They have chosen well, the cleansing rituals have been performed for us and the land, whenua it is called here, welcomes us to care for it," said Nani.

The waka turned to the beach for landing, and the Chief was the first man on the shore. He knelt on the beach and kissed the ground, relishing the sand that clung to his lips. They had done it. They had left disaster behind them, voyaged across the ocean and, with the guidance of the ancestors, found a place to build a new life. It had seemed such a daunting task to contemplate. He had questioned why he was chosen for such a task, but they had made it. Not one more life had been lost on the voyage, and they had gained a precious new life. More children would be born here, including the son of Tane, Marama, and Starman. Auspicious signs for displaced people.

Marama and Starman helped Nani ashore. Starman waded through the surf with Nani scooped up in his arms. They all couldn't stop grinning at each other; they had finally arrived. The voyagers were ecstatic and followed the Chief's lead, kissing the ground, rolling around on the sand, hugging the trees and each other, tears finally released.

Then came the practical tasks of unloading, securing the great canoes and setting up camp for the night. Fortunately, there were two caves just above the beach. Nani led them to the caverns where they could shelter for the night before finding a path to the new village site in the morning. People bustled around happily in the twilight hours. They were astonished by the foliage of the many trees, enjoying the feel of solid ground underfoot and laying out the sleeping mats for the first night on land. Perhaps it was the familiar presence of the ancestors that made them feel so welcome and so at home. All their fears evaporated the instant they set foot on the shore.

Fires crackled merrily inside the cave, and before long, there was hot food and drink to enjoy together. The camaraderie of the voyagers was as dense as the virgin forest. They had been through a lot together.

As night descended, Marama took Starman's hand and led him to the mouth the cave to look at the stars. Stars that were so plentiful it was a struggle to comprehend the enormity of the heavens.

"I know it is early, but can you help me find the approximate location of the island? I want to go to sleep tonight knowing where I am and where I came from," she said thoughtfully.

Starman showed her how to locate the island using different star groups. It was more complicated early in the evening, but once she knew where the island was, she was content.

"Will you show me where your home was one day? I want to know where you and our son will voyage when you return, even though I do not want to think about it yet," said Marama with a frown.

"Yes, of course, I will show you. I, like you, don't want to think about it just yet. I want us to enjoy being to-gether, being a family when our son is born and founding a new village," he said.

He gathered Marama in his arms, resting his head on hers, enjoying the familiar feel and smell of her against him. Marama leaned into his chest, marvelling that it now felt like home, being in his arms, the baby almost purring inside her. She was incredibly drawn to the land like she had been here before or was meant to be here. Marama could not wait to explore the hills and forests, discover plants, animals, and birds, and understand the stars.

Tonight, they needed sleep, so she took Starman's hand and led him to the sleeping mats where they could snuggle together and rest before exploring in the morning. Marama hugged Nani, found her tiny namesake for a cuddle, and kissed the Chief and Ari before retiring for the evening, allowing sleep to claim her body.

The voyagers sluiced off the salt and kissed the constant motion goodbye to become villagers again. They awakened early, eager to greet the dawn on the first day of their life in Aotearoa.

As the sun peeped above the horizon, it tinted the cloud formations with hues of pink. It revealed the deep, brooding, greenish-blue colour of the ocean, so different from where they came from but dazzling in its wild beauty.

The villagers were mesmerised, and as the dawn spread arms across the bay, reaching into the shadows, signalling to the night it was time for slumber, the red flowers of the pohutukawa (native Christmas trees) turned their heads to the sun and opened in all their glory.

Nani led the Chief and Marama on a path up the hill, and they watched the dawn from the plateau where they would build the new village. It was a reasonably steep climb, but the path they took wended its way back and forth through the trees and undergrowth because Nani, who had travelled the path already, knew precisely where to go. It was an awe-inspiring and spiritual moment for the three of them who had orchestrated what had once seemed an impossible task to save their people from extinction.

Before the sun's rays reached for them, they were suffused with the warmth of welcome from the spirits of the ancestors, and Earth Mother embraced them to her breast. They each took a handful of soil, a bowl of water from the stream and sat cross-legged on the plateau. They sang together a song of their voyage composed by the youngsters on the waka as the sunlight caressed their upturned faces.

Marama went to the bottom of the path, ready to lead the villagers to the plateau for the first time. Nani's voice rang through the air, calling the villagers to come, come to their ancestors, Chief, spirit guide and ancestral home. Marama answered Nani's call with her own as the villagers gathered behind her at the bottom of the hill. She collected young green ferns on the way back and held them in each hand, signalling to Nani that they heard her call and were coming to join them. Again, the people sang as they ascended the hill, first Nani and the Chief, then Marama and the villagers as they trekked upwards, the stream singing merrily beside them as they passed.

The morning air was crisp and fresh, the forest was verdant, Earth Mother was loamy in their nostrils, blood thrummed in veins, hearts beat in time with the singing, and the sense of returning home was palpable.

Marama paused at the entrance to the plateau as Nani sang of the ancestors who had chosen this location and their desire to reside with them here. The Chief danced a spectacular welcome with his taiaha, telling the story of the journey to reach this place in a fluid display of consummate skill.

As the Chief lay his weapon on the ground, he and Nani welcomed the villagers on behalf of the ancestors, greeting each person formally as they entered the village.

After the ceremony, there was much admiring of the view and the access to the springwater-fed stream. The Chief took the villagers on a site tour, showing them where the communal buildings would be placed and where they could build new whare for themselves.

People were astounded by the thought, detail and planning of the new village. The Chief explained the ancestors had put much thought and effort into the practicalities of the location and building their home.

The Chief had also dreamed of creating a palisade around the village to make it more defensible. He kept those thoughts to himself for now, as he wanted everyone to feel at home and just enjoy the vision of their future. There would be time to consider safety later.

Chief marked out the site of his whare and Nani's and invited the villagers to do the same. The sooner they occupied the site and made homes, the better, even if it was just a hearth and campsite for now.

268 ~ R. DE WOLF

People began bringing belongings up the hill from the canoes and placing them where their new whare would be. It was exciting to be making a permanent home after leaving behind so much.

The children were beside themselves, wanting to explore. First, they had to help with the tasks at hand and assist with preparing a communal meal. They ran up and down as fast as they could, fetched water from the stream, lit fires and worked hard to earn some free time later in the day.

Marama and Starman cleared her fish traps, offering the choice fish in each one to the sea, then reset them again. They sent the morning catch up the hill in baskets with some older boys before loading themselves up with as much communal gear as they could carry.

She listened to the birds singing as they climbed and mimicked their whistles as she walked, amusing Starman with her talent for imitating the sounds. The pair chatted as they hiked, still grinning at each other as the smaller birds flitted around them, twittering with tails spreading in fans, not afraid of them at all. They laughed, caught up in the excitement of building an entire village and a new home together. Their whare would be next to Nani, and they would still share a fire. Marama worked with Nani daily and did not want to be apart from her. Still, their own whare, for themselves and their children, made more practical sense, affording them all privacy.

After everyone had settled in, they shared a morning meal. They found everyone was famished, just as well they were on land where they could replenish supplies. Eventually, the children were let loose with instructions not to eat anything strange or wander too far. Nobody dreamed they would listen, but their parents hoped it would deter them from getting into too much trouble. Children raced off to explore before anyone could change their minds.

Marama was eager to climb to the top of the hill. She felt compelled to do so and asked Starman if he had time to accompany her. He smiled at her with mischief twinkling in his eyes.

"I do love it when you invite me to 'go walking' with you in the forest," he said. His suggestive tone earned a playful slap from Marama.

The rest of the village hooted at the love birds as they wandered into the forest and reminded them that there were innocent children out there who were not ready to see the birds and bees in action. Starman applauded before smacking Marama's bum to hurry her into the forest, causing giggles to erupt behind them as they ran off laughing.

The forest closed around them, deadening the sounds of activity they left behind and making them feel they might be the only people alive. Starman pulled Marama to him, feeling the rush of blood her proximity stirred in him. She pulled away reluctantly and grabbed his hand with a sense of urgency.

"Come on, we have to hurry to the top. Don't ask me why because I don't know myself," Marama said, turning away in a hurry.

Starman strode behind her, grateful for his long legs as Marama moved apace, driven to reach the top as quickly as possible. When they crested the final ridge, they breathed hard and sweat beaded Marama's brow.

Marama faced the ocean with a triumphant smile.

The whale jumped clear of the water, his hulking body forming a graceful arc that threw crystal droplets in the air around him. He sang his whale song. It reverberated through the core of her being in undulating waves. Marama's vision filled with the view from the whale's back, and she shared the baby's crowing with pleasure. A voice resonated in her mind. It was not like the spirits whispering but a strange, melodious singing that somehow made her understand.

"Thank you for playing with us, mother of my brother and rider. I need you to know me so when I return for the boy, he will be ready, and you will not be afraid," he said.

The whale rolled over in the water, displaying his unique markings to Marama. She committed the markings to memory, and then he returned to the depths.

Marama gasped as the whale left her, his voice still echoing in her mind. The baby leaked sadness at the departure of his friend into their shared body. Starman had his arms around them; he hadn't heard the conversation, but he saw the whale and sensed it was sending them a message. Bonding with a sea brother was a familiar and regular occurrence in his bloodline.

"Marama, tell me what happened?" he asked.

She looked at him, still slightly bewildered by the experience of having a whale communicate with her. Marama did not even know such a thing was possible until now.

"I, I am lost for words. I know the whale is the baby's guide, but it, it just talked to me. I'm not sure if it spoke or it all happened inside," she stammered. "It told me that I needed to know him. He showed me his markings, then told me that the boy must be ready, and I must not be afraid when he returns. Does this happen often in your family?"

Starman shook his head emphatically. He had never heard a story like this in either of the villages he had lived in. Kneeling in front of Marama, he kissed her belly before laying his head against it as if to hear his son.

"He will feel bereft that the whale has departed for the Southern Ocean. This is how we feel after experiencing the joy of bonding with our chosen guide. Everything will be well, my son. The whale will return to swim with you again, but you must rest and grow," he told the baby, holding his warm hand against Marama's belly.

Marama swallowed and blinked, moved by the sight of Starman on his knees, comforting their unborn son. She wondered what she had done to deserve such a good man and pulled him up to hug him. Marama wanted Starman to know how much she cared. She needed to tell him. Taking his face between her hands, Marama looked into his eyes, bright with intelligence but soft with tenderness.

"I must tell you something. When Tane was killed, I thought my heart shattered into more pieces than there are stars and that I would never be able to put it back together again. I only survived because I was driven to carry on by my thirst for vengeance, stirred by my clever Nani and Tane's spirit, who would not let me die. When we conceived the baby, even when we became a couple, I could not imagine life without Tane. When he left me again to let me live my mortal life properly, it hurt me. I felt like he took a piece of me with him. It pains me greatly to admit that he was right, but he was. Letting go of Tane has enabled me to be honest with myself, and the truth is that I love you with everything that is left of me, Starman.

"Maram-"

"No, let me finish. I don't feel like I deserve you sometimes." Marama held her fingers to his lips to staunch his protest. "What I want to say is important to me. You are strong and sensitive at the same time. Deeply spiritual in your own way. You give me respect, freedom, and I could not imagine anyone I would rather build a life with in this new land than you." Marama drew his lips to hers and sealed her declaration with a kiss. They were beginning a new life and would face whatever joys and trials awaited them in the future in Aotearoa together.

Glossary of Words

The fictitious characters in this novel travel from an un-specified island in Hawaiki, a region of the South Pacific. Words are allocated an abbreviated meaning in the context of the sentence in which they are used. Some words have multiple meanings and depths in other cultures that transcend the simple context used by the novel characters.

Aotearoa - Land of the long white cloud - New Zealand

Aue! - Exclamation of dismay

Haere mai - Come here

Haka - A ceremonial dance

Ika - Fish

Karakia - Prayer/incantation

Koka - Grandfather

Kuia - Respected elderly woman

Mana - Prestige

Manu - bird

Mokopuna - Grandchild

Pohutukawa - Metrosideros excelsa tree

Puku - stomach/belly

Taiaha - Long striking of thrusting weapon

Tapu - Forbidden/off limits/sacred

Tipuna/Tīpuna - Ancestor/s

Tohunga - Spiritual leader/medicine man/expert

Umu - Ground oven

Whanau - Family

Whare - House

Whenua - Land

Thanks & Acknowledgments

Writing a book is a process, and many people contribute to manifesting creativity. This book is the second edition and is published under the author's publishing banner and imprint. Testimony to how much one can learn in a few short years.

Taranga Kent, a poet and teacher, is also a first-rate proofreader. After reading the first edition, she presented the author with a list of corrections to make, for which she was grateful. Fellow writer Charlie Holland utilised her former publishing industry and study experience to assist with writing a new blurb - thank you. Evelyn Doyle was engaged to design a new cover for the book and bring her creative skills to the Spirit Voyager Series.

Since Guardians of the Ancestors was first published, the author studied with tutor Katrina Reedy at the TaiTech Writers Group at Tairāwhiti Technology Trust. Katrina and the group members' experience added many dimensions to the author's writing and increased her understanding of Te Ao Māori (the Māori world) - their wisdom was priceless. R. de Wolf is also a member of the Tairāwhiti Writers Hub and has the pleasure of working with Gillian Moon, Aaron Compton, Dorothy Fletcher and Karen Morris-Denby, to name a few. The Tairāwhiti Arts Festival has offered speaking engagements, stage performances and an opportunity to interact within the community - a remarkable artistic experience.

On a national level, the author has enjoyed the company and guidance of many talented writers as part of the New Zealand Society of Authors Central District Committee. Organising the Chatham Island Writers Retreat with Jackie Gurden in 2023 and meeting so many talented island writers RenaMay Hough, Deborah Goomes, Val Croon - too many to name them all, and the multi-talented mainland participants, was inspiring for the author. In 2024 de Wolf is participating in the launch of Te Kaituhi Māori with literary legend Witi Ihimaera, a Komiti of outstanding Māori writers and in conjunction with the NZSA - watch this space.

Writers are supported by their families and friends as they tap away and spend hours editing and agonising over their books. R. de Wolf pays tribute to her husband, Ieme de Wolf, who contributes to and puts up with the process. Family and friends turn up for book launches and promote the author's work. Special thanks to the Taiki E! whānau, sister Kerry, and friend Paula Kearns who are early readers.

The bookstores sell books - thanks to you all, especially Paper Plus in Gisborne. The author wants to recognise the readers who enjoy her work - you are why she writes.

Regina de Wolf-Ngarimu (Ngāti Porou, Te Whānau-ā-Apanui, Ngai Tahu, Ngāti Mutunga) is a Māori author and poet from the East Coast who loves kaimoana – penname **R. de Wolf**. She's published four novels and two poetry collections since 2020; *Guardians of the Ancestors* Book One of the six-part Pacific Fiction Adventure *Spirit Voyager Series*; Book Two, *The Future Weavers; Book* Three, *Brothers in Whalesong;* dystopian novel *The Goodness Algorithm; Poetry In a Pear Tree* and *Poetry In a Pohutukawa.* Three short stories, *Crushed Violet, Whale Brothers and The Hollow Mother,* were published in the Kaituhi Rāwhiti anthologies.

In 2022 she co-edited and published *Kaituhi Rāwhiti Two: Weaving of Words* with the Tairāwhiti Writers Hub, featuring over 40 writers connected to te Tairāwhiti. She also penned a short whakautu in 2023 for Ngā Kupu Wero *Penguin,* edited by Witi Ihimaera. Active in the writing community, Reg encourages rangatahi (youth) to kaumatua (seniors) to find their voice, preserve knowledge and publish commercial or private work.

The Future Weavers: Book 2

It's been seven years since Marama's people fled their Pacific island home and built a new life in Kāingatipu, Aotearoa (NZ). Starman and Kai, her man and son, will return to fulfil a prophecy. Marama is pregnant. She can't risk the baby or abandon her daughter and duties to travel with them.

While foraging, the women encounter unknown warriors seeking a foreign woman to give their chief a son. Marama's village is undefended. She lures the invaders away to save her people and allows the party leader, Rongo, to capture her.

Rongo's chief, Rangi, is pleased when Marama arrives in Rotowhā, and she seduces him. Marama cuckolds him into believing her child is his. The ancestors of Rotowhā have diverted Marama to their village with a purpose. Women have no status there, but Marama teaches them healing and reconnects them to Papatūānuku - the Earth Mother. Rangi's first love, Roimata, hates Marama on sight.

Discontent grows with Rangi's arrogance, abuse and his desire for bloodshed. To challenge Rangi is a death sentence, so his people suffocate under a blanket of fear. Desperate, Marama and the tohunga (spiritual leader) Piri risk their lives and form a covert alliance. Together, they uncover a complex web of lies, deception, greed and dark magic - in the past and present.

The future twists as the ancestors proffer solutions and a moral dilemma that challenges Piri and Marama's belief in the sanctity of life. When Atarangi, a weaver of malicious deeds, arrives in Rotowhā, events spiral out of control.

Milton Keynes UK
Ingram Content Group UK Ltd.
UKHW020647120424
440994UK00001B/19